The Lynx Hunter and other stories

The Lynx Hunter

and other stories

OWEN MARSHALL

John McIndoe

For Jacqueline, Andrea
and Belinda

Acknowledgement is made to
The Evening Standard, Islands, Landfall, Listener, More,
and *Untold* where some of these stories first appeared. A
number have also been broadcast by Radio New Zealand.

Published with the assistance of
the New Zealand Literary Fund

ISBN 0 86868 095 8

First published and printed 1987 by
John McIndoe Limited, 51 Crawford Street,
Dunedin, New Zealand.

Contents

One's real life is often the life one does not lead
— Oscar Wilde

Convalescence
In the Old City

O nly those who have experienced life there can know the feeling of the place; for such a city travels badly by words. An insect is active in the night there, between the paving stones of the old part of the city, and at first light sometimes I would see small mucus domes upon the cobbles. They made a brief defiance like fish eyes, then died beneath the bike wheels, the boots of passers by, the sun. And in that city there was a faint scent of the past — desperation and unrequited injuries — which mingled with the steam from the sewer covers, the smell of new baked saasi bread and sprays of blue, upland lilies carried to the sanctuary, and the sleeping breath of crowded people.

At dawn and dusk there is an awkward turning: pretence fails, and sensed in the brief hiatus as one state gives way to another is sadness for things seen as they are. I prefer to be alone at both these times, or if in company to avoid the eyes of others. In the old city the death of a day or a night was a vulnerable time; one rhythm lost, another not quite begun. A time when symptoms of illness reappeared and achievements seemed most trivial.

I was there for a month only, a little less, restricted by convalescence to a very limited patrol; the hotel, its view and acquaintances, the labiniska and the narrow streets surrounding. So I can't claim any general knowledge of the country, just the experience of a short time in the old city.

Mine was a small hotel, and the only other regular guest who was around much during the day was a Polish engineer. I didn't see his name written, but my guess is Debicki, Moritz Debicki. He came from Kalisz. I have never been to Poland; never known Polish people except for this one acquaintance. My expectation, based on films and books, was that Poles were histrionic and libidinous, full of poetic melancholy and the hopeless courage of lost causes. Yet Debicki was very practical and brisk. He had come south as an engineer to work in the heavy industry of the new city, and because it was the time of union agitation he had little to do and was on half pay until work could begin again. He found a way of turning circumstance to his advantage. He obliged with plumbing and mechanical work at the labiniska, and for the family tannery a few blocks from the hotel. The smell of the tannery remained with him after this work. Of course he was paid under the table by both concerns, to supplement his half pay, and was pleased with his resourcefulness.

I wasn't well enough to go far from the hotel, and Moritz Debicki came in to talk to me in my room many days, or sat with me a while on the ramp by the old stables which held the shade. He was a foreigner too, but more familiar with the place than I, for he had lived there for almost two years and could speak the language. He had a wish to be helpful to me — alone in the old city. Also Moritz liked to use his English, which was surprisingly good. He didn't like to waste opportunities, and if I was quiet too long from fatigue, or thought, he would prompt me to conversation again by starting up himself. 'The next day I am going to do work in the machineries of the tannery,' or 'Men and women in this country: both of them are not modern in thinking. They live in the history of their country altogether.'

I was glad of Moritz Debicki. I appreciated his practical nature, his interest in me a stranger convalescing in the hotel, and his courtesy in regard to nationality. As a Pole perhaps he considered pride in country to be everywhere a significant thing. Often when he came to visit me he would offer some knowledge of New Zealand as a greeting: a gift of his research somewhere in a city which cannot have groaned with information of Aotearoa. I hadn't the resources or freedom to repay in kind, except to praise Chopin, and the charge of the Polish cavalry against the German tanks. Moritz told me with pleasure for both our countries that New

Zealand's export trade to Poland was greater than to Spain, Sweden, Austria or Yugoslavia.

Midday was a sour sweat in summer; hot, still, and the fumes of the industries in the new city drifted into the irregular streets on the hill. The men left their sidewalk chairs along the wall of the labiniska I could see from my room. They took their tall tankards inside, away from the heat and the pollution of the new industries they despised; inside, where windows were closed.

Late in the afternoon however a fresh world was begun. By four the heat was such that it defeated itself, thus the cooler air came flowing down from the hills and the mountains behind them, and the poisons of the new industries no longer reached the old part of the city. Moritz said that the local name for the cool air meant snow breath, and when it came the decorous men brought their tankards out from the labiniska and took their seats again; women moved about the narrowing streets; the hotel cook who had a lazy eye talked loudly to his staff of one.

Moritz Debicki was fond of schnapps; I never developed the taste for it. He would bring the bottle when he came to see me, and two small glasses with very thick bottoms. He might preface his visit by saying that he knew Taupo to be the largest lake in New Zealand, or that our kiwi was an oddity of nature which I should explain to him. There was a sense of unreality concerning my country when I heard it described in formal tit-bits by a Polish engineer in a hotel room above the sloping streets in the old city. As I might in ignorance have talked of prayer wheels in Tibet, or the red fields of Tuscany. Outside my window was a plant box. The grey dirt had shrunk from the wooden sides in the heat, and there were no flowers. Moritz would stand at the open window in the evening and rest his schnapps bottle in the window box. He could see the men on their chairs along the wall, and he scorned them for their lack of ambition. Moritz was resolved to be a fully qualified mechanical engineer within a year, and then return, he said, to Poland and marry a virgin of good family. There were some very good virgins and families in Kalisz, he assured me, which was after all a city of some 85,000 people.

When it was becoming dark and the snow breath had saved the old city again, sometimes the men along the wall of the labiniska

9

would begin to sing. Songs not at all boisterous, but polite and reflective. As night came on a son or daughter would be sent by the women and stand respectfully at a distance to remind a singer of his family. And the father would leave his seat along the wall, leave his quiet, repetitive singing, and go home with the child sent for him.

In the old city it seemed to me that the electricity was different from electricity in other places, although the pragmatist will tell you that it can't be so: the light lacked penetration and was very yellow. Moritz told me that it was because the city supply was overloaded and all the apparatus second rate. I recall the singing as night came, the weak, yellow light of windows and corner lamps, and the stink of the new city moved away by the cool air of the mountains. But I don't pretend to know more than these appearances of the place, for I was there a little less than a month, and restricted mainly to the hotel and the immediate streets by not being well. I have often disparaged those who pronounce upon a place with authority after some superficial experience of it, and who have no understanding of the life and sustaining prejudices of people there, so I won't name the country or city. Yet I was there; saw the things which I describe, as you might see them yourself if you cared to. Yet nothing is ever quite the same, even in such an old city, and the earth within the window box may not crack in just that pattern again, and Moritz Debicki is unlikely to be still in that hotel where I saw him arrested for theft.

Moritz would stand at the window, or sit on the other iron bed in my room, and talk to me in his effective English. His face was lively and he would tend his moustache with the thumb and forefinger of his left hand. His interest in people was sociological rather than personal, it seemed to me: he talked of groups and classes, not individuals, to a degree that was unusual. The striking factory workers were a fascination to him, their habits and intentions, but only as a body; he had no friends among them. He knew the characteristics of the traditional minorities of the old city's population, and explained to me the utterly different lives of married and unmarried women. Yet when I praised the expressive eyes of the maid at the labiniska, he said he hadn't noticed, but that almost certainly she would be Croatian.

Our acquaintance remained a slightly formal one: talks in my room, or less often on the ramp of the stables, an occasional walk in the evenings along the streets of the old city, or a visit to the labiniska where we seemed to inhibit the regulars so that they didn't sing. Moritz and I maintained a certain reserve — on my part because I liked him but was wary of rapid intimacy which might prove a mistake. I still needed a good deal of quiet and rest. And also it was so obviously a temporary coincidence. A Polish engineer from Kalisz working in the new industries before returning to a virgin of good family, and a Kiwi teacher taking an unintended convalescence on his European tour.

Almost always I ate at the hotel, and not just to keep expenses down. Eating places were few in the old city; the locals ate at home, and it was not a tourist city to any special extent. The spread of the industries in the new city and the priorities of the government discouraged anything frivolous or deliberately appealing. The hotel food was all I needed, or felt like. The large meal was late in the evening, when the snow's breath had come, for even in summer we usually had a heavy soup. I have seen the cook adding the bowl of blood late in its cooking — displaying the addition with pride. 'It is known an excellent goodness,' Moritz told me.

On my last Tuesday I finished my soup as the two policemen arrived in the dining room. There were seven guests including myself. The police were looking for Moritz Debicki, but he was working late at one of his under the table jobs. Both men were noticeably handsome, dark, set off well by their green and black uniforms. The police in that city all seemed possible leading men; perhaps they were chosen for appearance rather than stature or skills; perhaps it was just the effect of the uniform. The senior man remained in the dining room to smoke, while the other policeman went out and waited in the foyer. Nothing was said between them; either it was planned beforehand, or their customary procedure. The hotel guests did not linger after the meal, and I was the last to go to my room. The policeman in the foyer smiled at me as I went up the stairs. It seemed disloyal to Moritz not to make some effort to warn him, and I stood by my window as if I would have the opportunity to signal to him on the cobbled street. I had little conviction though; for all I knew it could be a matter of some technicality. I learnt practically nothing of the language in my time there.

Moritz Debicki didn't pass my window, and he was arrested in the foyer as he returned to the hotel. I heard the first, quick words, then the louder protestations of Moritz. To go down was all that I could do; my uncomprehending presence was the only support that I could offer him. One policeman gripped Moritz firmly by the jacket as they argued. Their three voices echoed in the hotel foyer, but no one else came out; the hotel was quiet everywhere except the foyer.

'Is this necessary?' I said. It sounded absurd even as I said it, for who was I to stand in the entrance of a hotel in the old city and question in English the actions of authority? The policemen regarded me, but didn't reply.

'I am so arrested for robbery of the tannery', said Moritz. The police began to urge him from the hotel foyer into the street. The grip on his jacket pocket was maintained, but there was no sign of hand-cuffs or guns. Moritz called to me over his shoulder at the doorway. 'In your country would not occur this bungle of justice,' and as I had been addressed the senior policeman paused to nod at me.

I was ashamed for Moritz: his casual clothes shabby in contrast with the smart green and black of the police. The shabbiness was accentuated by his humiliation. I was ashamed for myself too — for my inability to be of any influence for his benefit in the situation, for my witness of his humiliation. They walked closely together across the uneven cobbles and past the labiniska wall where the singers sat quietly. I could see no car in the twilight. Moritz was still held by the pocket. One of his shoulders was lower than the other because of that grip, and his shoes were worn at the heels.

In that way was my acquaintance at the hotel in the old city taken away, and I went myself two days later. The police wouldn't let me see Moritz Debicki before I left the old city and its country. I never discovered if Moritz was really a thief, and if I would feel either of us changed because of it. I have only facts; those things that happen and then break off, as facts do, without the moral or symmetry of a story. Perhaps the justice he received was indeed a bungle; perhaps he was a thief.

Good fortune to Moritz Debecki. I hope he continues to enjoy his schnapps, that he finishes his training, that he returns to Polish Kalisz to marry a virgin of good family. Yet all I'm sure of are the facts of the place and the experience. You may see such things yourself if you go there. Often when not well, I sat at the window and watched dawn in the old city — that turning, honest time. At dawn the triangle of our lives is glimpsed; three equal, sloping sides of time and change and death. I saw on the cobble stones the mucus bubbles made by insects in the night, and watched steep houses come up against the sky.

Punt
And Winter Day

N eil said he wanted a comfort stop. We had been travelling for nearly two hours. Kevin turned towards the coast; up over a miniature wooden bridge and down a shingle road still dampened from the frost. The river was unable to maintain a clear channel to the sea; blocked by a bar it lay in loops and sheets of dark water on a flat landscape. A minor river which we didn't recognise, and which was unable to break free. Neil clambered awkwardly from the car, and went off the distance his modesty required.

There are some South Island days, winter days, with no wind at all, rather bird calls in the air, and after frost the bright, calm sun shows all the various greens and yellows, and the single whiteness of the snow there on the mountains cut against the sky. When a whistle can be heard over two miles, clear, but with a tinge of echo that indicates the distance.

Neil still stood absorbed, facing away. The back of his blue suit was creased by travel, and his thin neck rose like a cabbage stalk to a head with dry, sparse hair. 'What a bore. What a bloody old woman he is,' said Kevin quietly, but with vehemence. 'Why did he have to come, Laurie?' Laurie only shrugged and smiled. 'If he talks anymore today about his computer accounts system I'll brain him. Yak, yak, yak all the time.'

'He and his wife are big in the Cactus and Succulent Society,' said Laurie, knowing the reaction.

'Is that a fact! Jesus. All those girls in his department you know, and I've heard he hasn't screwed one of them. Not one of them.'

'Perhaps the criteria for promotion are different for salesmen and accountants,' said Laurie. Kevin laughed with us. He felt quite flattered.

'You know what I mean,' he said. He wandered off the road towards the river, drawn like a boy towards the water.

'I'll stretch my legs too, now we're here,' I said. Laurie walked slowly with me. He raised his arms and yawned. 'I thought the talks went well enough,' I said. 'It seems to me this merger could be on.'

'The Board's already made up its mind I think, irrespective of any report we give, so we may as well justify their opinion. There's no reason after all why it shouldn't work.' Laurie gave me his knowing grin. 'You and I'll get together on it,' he said. I could feel the delicate warmth of the winter sun on my face and hands. From the coast, out of sight behind the estuary and the final bar, came the sound of the swell. The rush up the beach muted even in that still, winter air, and the pause as the waves drained away.

Neil caught up with us. He had the self-conscious smile with which he sought fellowship. 'What remarkable weather,' he said. He had a small face and fussy moustache. His nose was reduced and curved like a parrot's beak. He had shaved badly as usual and the sun showed long hairs beneath his left jaw line. 'The bliss of rural calm,' he said. 'So very different from the office, where Titans slave and the world is put to rights.'

'There's a boat here,' called Kevin. He was along the bank, on slightly higher ground. 'Look at this.' A white punt lay upside down beside the rushes. It was tied to a waratah sunk deep in the bank. The oars lay like chopsticks beside it. 'Duck shooters I suppose,' said Kevin. In the far lagoon, close to the beach, we could see several tattered mai-mais. Kevin turned the punt over and began pushing it on its flat bottom towards the water. 'Come on,' he said.

'We haven't time to be fooling around,' said Laurie.

'Just a quick break.' Kevin untied the punt. His enthusiasm and energy involved us in the launching. The punt seemed all buoyancy: it bobbed and skidded on the water as if held up by surface tension. Kevin's weight then mine made it more sober.

'What's the point,' said Laurie, but he climbed carefully in, and Neil followed with self-conscious comradeship.

15

The punt sank low in the water with the four of us. Kevin and I rowed. The oars rattled; the punt moved over the still water in the sun, and when we rested water ran from the blades on to the malleable surface of the estuary. The drops were clear, but the water in total was stained brown, and the bottom below could be seen as if through a beer bottle. Weeds combed out on the estuary bed, ridges of mud and sand were pressed close by the weight of water, and occasionally there was a log or branch, dim beneath the brown water like old ivory.

Kevin and I rowed up to the one span bridge: we could reach up and hold the deck without standing. We rowed back again, with the rattle of the oars and the dripping water sounding clearly. There was a certain incongruity: the four of us in business suits, the only people in that landscape, crowded in the white, laden punt on the brown estuary of an unknown river.

'It's very relaxing,' said Neil. 'As a boy I had quite a lot to do with boats because we lived at Waitati on the coast.'

'Some other time,' said Kevin.

'Pull back over,' said Laurie. 'We'd better start on our way. I've got a good deal still to do on the report when we get back.'

'I wasn't convinced with their presentation of the market compatibility between the two companies,' said Neil. No-one replied. Kevin sagged his face comically at me when Neil couldn't see.

Kevin held the rushes to keep the punt close to the bank as Laurie stepped out, then Laurie took the mooring rope while the rest of us came ashore. We stood in the sun and looked over the estuary. The sound of the gulls carried from the coast, and there was a persistent piping from the mudflats though no birds were visible. 'I would say they shoot swan and all here,' said Kevin. 'It's a fair stretch of water.' The punt was still, and Laurie let the rope fall so that he could take a handful of grass and wipe mud from the welts of his shoes. The punt veered a little, and the rope slid into the water. 'You've let the rope go in,' said Kevin. The rope lay on the surface for a moment then began to sink: the descent was in soft undulation like a ribbon in the air. At first there seemed no risk of losing the punt. Laurie was more interested in his shoes than securing it. Kevin put out a leg, touched the boat clumsily and moved it further away. The punt rocked in the still, dark water; wrinkles spread from it which only emphasized the solidity of the estuary. Kevin held his arm out. 'Bugger,' he said. He held his arm out more to estimate the distance than in hope that he might reach the boat. He stuck his backside out and reached further. The punt was a foot or two beyond arm's reach. One oar trailed in the tobacco-stained water, drawn gradually through the rowlock by the boat's movement. The punt drifted slowly towards the lagoon, still close to the bank. 'Bugger the thing,' said Kevin.

'We could reach it with an oar,' said Neil. We had no oar and the comment was irritating. The punt was like a pet that didn't wish to be caught; that tantalises by remaining just out of reach when it could easily escape altogether. Neil went back along the bank to where the hilt of the waratah stuck out of the higher ground. He took hold of it, one hand over the other, and lifted his head up from his crouch in the effort to raise the waratah. His parrot's nose wrinkled. 'Not a hope,' he said. The punt arced with slow grace, but was still close. The oar trailed like a broken arm, drawn a little longer into the water.

'That oar's going to fall out,' said Kevin. We surveyed the bank for something which would reach out to the punt. There was nothing. Only silt and mud and water and reeds, and pasture stretching away with vigorous yellow-orange rushes in the dips and channels. And an amazing blue winter heaven with no shimmer of heat to affect its clarity; and the mountains cut against the sky. The oar slipped from the rowlock and without obvious impetus glided away from the punt. Both were now moving further from the shore, held up on the dark, firm water and drifting towards mudbanks which lay and glistened like a barely glimpsed dark intestine on the estuary bend.

'That's that, I'm afraid,' said Laurie.

'Damn,' said Kevin. 'How's anyone supposed to retrieve the thing when it drifts off like that.'

'It's just one of those things,' said Laurie. He was bored with the punt, the estuary, the situation. Laurie was usually bored unless there was a sufficient audience to challenge his talents. The landscape held no prospect of advancement.

The punt reached the mudbar, and we could tell when it grounded for it stopped its slow pirouette and lay three-quarters on to our view, absolutely flat and still to us at that distance; as if painted there the colour of an oyster shell against the dark mud and the looping estuary behind. 'It'll be okay there, when the owner comes he'll find it there all right. It's not as if it's drifted out to sea entirely' I said.

'Right,' said Laurie. We found it easy to absolve ourselves from responsibility: except for Neil.

'Yes, but it's our fault,' he said. 'We should've left it alone and now it's gone, and the next rain or even the next tide might lose it altogether.'

'So what,' said Kevin.

'We'll call at the first farm house we go past. Leave a message and apology,' said Laurie. We looked over the flat, immediate landscape; the raised approaches to the wooden bridge.

'What farm house?' said Neil.

'The first we see. It's not Outer Mongolia you know, Neil.'

'That's right,' said Kevin.

Neil had a lack of convenient common sense; it was one of the exasperating things about him. 'Maybe we could walk out to it,' he said.

'Do me a bloody favour,' said Kevin. 'In our gear; at this time of year? Don't let this sun fool you. It'll freeze your balls off, that water.'

'It's an obligation.' Neil's parrot nose was set resolutely.

'Look Neil,' said Laurie. 'If there was any reasonable way in which we could return the damn boat, we would. As I said before we'll call in at the first farm house we see and tell them about the boat. Even if they're not the owners themselves they'll be able to pass the message on. You know what these country districts are like. Isn't that the sensible thing to do?' Laurie always knew the sensible thing to do. Neil didn't.

'I'll just have a look at that sand-bank,' he said.

'Mud-bank,' Kevin said.

'That's right,' I said.

I don't think Neil had listened to anything that Laurie had been saying. He went off down the bank towards the curving intestine of mud and silt on which the punt had come to rest. 'Don't be all bloody day. We're going soon,' said Laurie. We stood and watched Neil.

He took off his shoes and socks. He started along the mud-bank. We could hear the loving suck of the mud even on his first few steps.

'He's hurt his foot,' said Kevin. Neil hobbled back. 'He's taken off his trousers,' said Kevin. Neil put his shoes on again, and turned back over the mud: no trousers, no socks, but suit coat and tie. A white leg was drawn high on each step, and then sank deep into the mud. Our ease and his discomfort at a distance made him appear the more ridiculous. Kevin was delighted; he watched and laughed.

'Dozy beggar,' said Laurie. Neil held out his arms at times to give counter-weight and balance as he struggled to draw his feet out of the mud. His commitment made us laugh the more.

'Jesus, I bet that's cold.' Neil sucked and wobbled through the mud: he waved his arms for balance and his shirt tail hung in a pale crescent. Behind him the mud newly raised to the surface was darker, and marked his track. Kevin continued a commentary on progress, not for the benefit of Laurie and myself, but as emphasis for his own amusement. 'He's found the other oar,' he said. The oar made Neil's task more difficult, and twice he fell forward and we heard the oar smack on the mud. 'He's down again. Ah, Jesus, it's better than a play.' Neil could hear the laughter I suppose. He reached the punt at last: tried to push it off and climb aboard in one action. It wasn't easy in the holding mud. 'Look, he's down again. Ah — ahh, Jesus me. Now it's turned round again: it's stuck again. Look at that. Bugger me though.'

The punt was free finally, and Neil in it. He rowed a twisting course up the estuary towards us. Kevin was disappointed that there were no further misfortunes, but he tied the punt up with a good grace, and even retrieved Neil's trousers and socks, while Neil washed as best he could at the edge of the water. He reeked of innumerable things that had been locked beneath the mud, compounding their odours for eventual release. He had a cut on the instep of his left foot. He sat sideways in the back seat of the car, with the door open, and inspected his foot carefully before putting on his socks. He was shivering despite the bright sun.

Laurie threw Neil's misshapen shoes into the car boot. 'What a stink,' he said. 'We've been here over an hour, do you know that?' I sat with Neil in the back seat: I felt I had deserved it. It's a mistake to think we always respect our friends, or despise those we laugh at. Our friends are often too much like ourselves for admiration, and those with whom we have little in common may be models for reluctant conscience. The primeval fragrance of the mud settled amongst us. Kevin wrinkled his face. Smears of mud were drying on Neil's skin, turning grey. Mud was even in the pouch of his ear, and a little gathered wetly at the corner of his eye.

'The mud was exceedingly cold,' he said, 'as Kevin suggested, but strangely it wasn't much deeper way out than by the shore.'

'Is that a fact though,' said Kevin. Neil began a precise recitation of his rescue of the punt: his parrot nose shivering in profile. In front Kevin opened and closed his mouth in wordless mimicry.

We crossed the bridge. The estuary was unchanged behind us; a snapshot of smooth water, yellow and green flats scarcely raised above it, and the sea lying low at a distance.

The Ace of
Diamonds Gang

As our past recedes we can see only occasional pennons on the high ground, which represent the territory traversed between. So the Ace of Diamonds Gang seems my full boyhood before the uncertainty of adolescence. I recall no peculiar origin; like the heroes of history it arose when it needed to be there.

Always the special moment was when we put on our masks. The triangle of white handkerchief over the lower face, and the red diamond that we'd stamped on with the oil paints that belonged to Bernie's mother. There was frisson as each known face became strangely divided. Not handkerchiefs with red diamonds smudged did we acquire, but anonymity, confederacy, a clear exception to approved society. After Boys' Brigade was a favourite time; when lanyards and Christianity had been dispensed with, we would rendezvous in the centre of the old macrocarpa hedge to become the Ace of Diamonds Gang. The night would be moonlit perhaps and we would move off in dispersed formation, keeping in touch by drifting whistles and calls of birds extinct except within the diamond lands. Like wraiths we went said Bernie once. He read a lot did Bernie. Like wraiths, the Ace of Diamonds Gang: if Ashley's farting didn't give us all away.

The Ace of Diamonds Gang was rather like that; subject in practice to mundane deficiences which threatened the ideal. Ashley's wind, Bernie's glasses and Hec Green having to be in by nine o'clock every night, were the sorts of things. A certain power of imagination was necessary, but for 13-year-olds the source of such power is inexhaustible. We never spent much time in explicit definition of the Gang however — each had his own motivation, his own vision of the Ace of Diamonds Gang, and when we struck in that small town each of us gloried in a quite separate achievement. Dusty Rhodes insisted that the gang be used to intensify his wooing of Anna Nicholson who had the best legs in the school. It was love all right. After watching Anna at the swimming sports, Dusty had a hormone headache so severe that he was away for three days. The Ace of Diamonds Gang picketed Anna Nicholson's front garden sometimes, and when she came back from music practices called from the bushes and tossed acorns up to her window. Dusty considered this a normal form of courtship, and the rest of us had not sufficient experience to suggest alternatives. When Anna's father came out with torch and fury, we would drift wraith-like deeper into the shrubbery, not of course from fear, but to give him a taste of the menacing elusiveness of the Ace of Diamonds Gang when true love was thwarted. Dusty could never understand why Anna Nicholson didn't fall for him. The unbearable passion of first love rarely has any relevance to the response of the other party.

For Bernie and me the Ace of Diamonds Gang was more a life warp to escape from being 13 years old in a provincial town; a chance to conjure heroism, to strike a pose, to create mysteries in which to dwell. We cut the backs off some Christmas cards, and stamped them with the red diamond. We left one at the scene of each of our exploits, just as in the books we read. The senior sergeant would pin them on his incident board we were sure, and his staff would attempt to work out a modus operandi.

So it was something of a let down to return to Seddon Park weeks after we had painted challenges there, and find the Ace of Diamonds card still there, weathered on the side of the cricket shed. 'They've given up, that's what,' said Dusty.

'That's it all right. They've given up,' said Ashley.

'Perhaps it's still under surveillance,' said Bernie. It was a good word — surveillance, but even it could not impose conviction in that warm morning with the playing fields dipping to the willows, and a harrier club spread in the distance.

'We haven't actually done much lately,' admitted Ashley, who was sitting downwind a little. 'As a gang I mean.' We lay in the grass, shading our eyes with our hands, and attempting to justify the lack of daring in recent excursions of the Ace of Diamonds Gang.

Dusty suggested we spend time drilling a hole in the girls' changing sheds, but the rest of us wanted a cause of greater daring and less obvious connection with our own interest. 'My father told me Jorgesson poisoned Mrs Elder's Alsatian because it kept him awake at night,' said Ashley. Jorgesson ran the second-hand yard, and his emnity could be relied on. He had cuffed Dusty's head for cheek, and once set the police on us after seeing us on the stacks of the timber yard. And he gave us wretched prices for any lead or copper we scrounged because he had the monopoly as the only scrap dealer in town. Sometimes we retrieved the stuff from his yard and sold it to him twice over to gain a fair price by simple addition, but even retaliatory dishonesty didn't remove our resentment.

'Hey, Jorgesson,' repeated Dusty. To defy Jorgesson was grand enough to be a reaffirmation of the principles of the Ace of Diamonds Gang, and Dusty agreed to hold in abeyance further collective effort to seduce Anna Nicholson, and the spy-hole in the sheds.

'Let's raid the place and leave a calling card,' said Hec. 'Poison him perhaps.'

'Wraith-like we shall strike,' intoned Bernie, raising a small, clenched fist. 'Strike and vanish, vengeance accomplished; the Ace of Diamonds Gang.' It was Bernie who usually provided the linguistic motifs for the gang.

'Christ, yes,' said Hec, 'but I'll have to be back by nine remember.'

In the fastness of the macrocarpa we met on Wednesday evening; looked out into the soft, eternal twilight of summer. We linked thumbs to make our pledge and put on our Ace of Diamonds masks. Just a handkerchief and a change of mind. The mantle of secret brotherhood then fell upon us — oh, it was fish Christians in the catacombs, the Black Hand, Jacobites, the Scarlet Pimpernel. It was the League of Spartacus, the Boxers: it was Kipling's bazaar. I felt a small part of history's perpetual alternative as we ran through the Marlborough evening.

Jorgesson's was in that part of the town which was never very busy; off the main street and down towards the warehouses. On one side of his yard was a panelbeater's, on the other a vacant section, then the timber yard. When night came all such lands reverted to the domain of the Ace of Diamonds Gang. We scaled the stepped pyramids of the timber yard, and made inventory of Jorgesson Traders. It resembled a field hospital in a desperate war of machines: the corpses and the parts heaped in rough classification as they came in. The ground was toxic and stained with oils, rust and the juices of dismembered machines. There were heaps of taps like discarded hands, radiators, bumpers, fan units, old bricks, used sinks, ceramic fire surrounds, short blocks, coppers, windows, roofing iron, bottle castles in green and brown, heaps of worn tyres like bitter, dark intestines. Amidst all the obsolescence were a few new kitset patio chairs assembled by Jorgesson during his quiet times. Much of the stock was exposed to take its chances beneath the spartan sky; a second category lay in an open-sided shed and its progressively diminishing lean-tos. We knew that the most precious and portable items festooned Jorgesson's army hut, so that it was a labyrinthine progress for him to make the short journey from his desk and cashbox to the door.

There seemed a dim light from the hut as we watched from our battlements. 'He must still be there,' said Hec. Ashley perfumed the night in response to heightened and unexpected tension.

'But we'll still go,' I said.

'We should reconnoitre in strength,' advised Bernie. His glasses glinted a moment in the last light of the evening. We steadied ourselves on the timber, and locked our thumbs again in pledge.

So did we move wraith-like across the rough section between the timber yard and Jorgesson's, scouts taking post then others fading forward. We hand-cupped each other over the fence, drew up Hec as the last, and stood amongst Jorgesson's darkened possessions. The one window in the army hut showed light like the pale yellow yolk of a battery egg. It was above head height and we pushed a drill chassis close to the wall — inch by inch to reduce the noise of the high, iron wheels on the gravel and scattered artifacts of Jorgesson's yard.

Jorgesson was lying on the floor by the door, or rather Jorgesson was lying on a woman who was on the floor by the door. It was the only space available; the one strip for the door to open and the clients to stand amidst Jorgesson's plunder. Jorgesson and his love seemed accustomed to the position, for without needing to look behind her, the woman reached an arm to brace herself on a stack of long life batteries, and Jorgesson's trousers hung conveniently on the impressive tines of a wapiti head behind him.

The apparent irrationality of sex is a vast humour to the young. Jorgesson had no electricity in his hut, and the low, angled light from a small Tilly was unflattering: single tendons jerking behind Jorgesson's great knees were picked out, and the wrinkles behind his head, and how flat his back-side was in fact. Of the woman there was little more than the one practical arm, and her toes, separate and tumescent as facets in the Tilly light.

'He's doing her,' said Dusty. 'He really is.' His voice had qualities of awe and relief; as if after all the furtive talk, the innuendo, the chapter endings, the fade-outs, he was reassured that the act itself was not a myth. Jorgesson was doing it before his eyes. 'Jesus,' said Dusty.

'Yea,' said Hec.

Jorgesson was unaware of any need to prolong his performance for our education. He slipped to the side, cleverly angling one leg between a brass fire guard and a Welsh dresser. He drew a rug about his love, and laid his bare arm upon it to stroke her hair. A candle sheen seemed on his arm in the localised Tilly light, and his face was all Punch features as he talked, stark in relief and shadow. Braces were a limp bridle from the wapiti, and the love's toes had coalesced with the passing of ecstasy.

The Ace of Diamonds Gang found an aftermath of restful affection disappointing. Dusty grumbled on the drill perch, and Bernie began hand signals of obscure intrigue. We had come to punish Jorgesson, and his pleasure would provide another cause. We withdrew to the darkness of Jorgesson's open shed to plan our assault. 'Have you got the card?' said Bernie. It was my turn: my turn to spike it, as Bernie said. I could feel it in my top pocket.

They gave me two minutes to creep around to the front of Jorgesson's hut, and there I took the card from my pocket and the brass pin from the other side of my shoe. As I fixed it to the centre of Jorgesson's door, fellow partisans began their attack: stones cascaded upon the roof, Ashley ran towards me down the flank of the hut banging the boards with a length of piping, Dusty and Hec gave their wolf howls, Bernie beat a scoured copper in sonorous rhythm. The Ace of Diamonds Gang had released its terror.

I could hear also a sudden commotion as Jorgesson tried to rise from amongst his possessions to counter-attack. I had joined the others in a race for the gate when Jorgesson seemed to smite down the door and was behind us, like a black jumping jack with profanity as his sparks. His voice was husky with passion, and rage gave him an initial impetus — but we were prepared. Fled; the white masks and red diamonds flowing in and out of colour as we raced past the street lights. We were our own audience, struck by the audacity of the Ace of Diamonds Gang; avengers, raiders, sentinels, even if Bernie had to carry his glasses as he ran and had trouble keeping up. 'Wait on, wait on,' he kept calling, which impaired our wraith-like progress.

Jorgesson gave up though, once we reached the Sherwood of the timber yard. It was darker amid the stacks and he had no intimate knowledge of the trails there. He halted and sent in a verbal pack of bastards, buggers and sods to harry us on our way.

'Go home shagger,' shouted Hec.

'Serve him right,' said Dusty, but his tone was one more of envy than impartial justice.

'Remember the Ace of Diamonds Gang,' called Bernie hauntingly. We joined thumbs on one of the stacks when Jorgesson was gone, and enjoyed the exaggeration of what we had done: except Hec, who had to go straight home and risk being belted.

The depleted Ace of Diamonds Gang maintained its identity through the streets and short cuts from the timber yard to its macrocarpa headquarters; each scout call an echoing clearance. Yet after victory over Jorgesson there was arrogance rather than caution in our progress, and in the macrocarpa, darker than the blue, summer night, we put aside our masks and our greater lives with unspoken dismay.

In my room I folded my mask and placed it within the fuselage of the Spitfire Mk II; the special place. I began to undress, and as I pulled my jersey over my head I could feel my library card still in the shirt pocket from the afternoon. Except that it wasn't the library card; it was the Ace of Diamonds sign made out of the back of a

Xmas card, and as I recognised it there was a flux of all my stomach, and blood pumping up my eyeballs, hair follicles quickening all over my skin, falling electrical cadences of primeval terror through the matter of the brain. It was the library card I had pinned on the door of Jorgesson's army hut in the second-hand yard. The Ace of Diamonds Gang had witnessed his secret love, had interrupted it, had taunted him from the night sky and the timber stacks — and I had left my library card pinned to the centre of his door to avow responsibility.

I dreamt of Jorgesson's retribution during the night, starting up in abrupt horror at each climax revealed. Jorgesson in the Headmaster's study when I was sent for, Jorgesson waiting in the shadows with an old sickle from stock, Jorgesson fingering a garroting cord beneath the swaying pines, Jorgesson at the door with my library card and asking to see my father.

That's how it happened. I had just taken a mouthful of Toad in the Hole when I saw through the kitchen window an unnaturally tidy Jorgesson coming past the geraniums. There was a bulge in his pocket which could have been a garroting cord, and his Punch head was tilted to accommodate a paisley tie. I have always since hated geraniums and paisley patterns. A geranium is a coarse, disease ridden plant with a flare of animosity and paisley resembles a slide of pond water beneath a microscope. Even Toad in the Hole has never been quite the same again. My father and Jorgesson spent time in sombre conversation, and although I couldn't catch the words I could see on Jorgesson's face successive expressions of contained outrage, reasonableness, social duty to parents of evil children. My library card passed from Jorgesson to my father; the indisputable proof of a tale too rich to be denied.

My father punished me with the razor strop, and rang the parents of each friend I had unhesitatingly betrayed. It was the end of the Ace of Diamonds Gang. It was the end of wraith-like sorties into the consciousness of our town; it was the end of silhouettes upon the timber stacks, of thumbs clasped to pledge the redress of make shift grievances. It was the end of free imagination, and of boyhood perhaps.

The Lizard Again

Alan.

I'm in here.

Oh there you are then.

I said just now I was in here.

I couldn't get a case of apricots at the mart.

You wouldn't on a Monday. There's nothing been transported the day before.

Of course.

Maybe tomorrow.

I saw the silver candelabra.

I can't think of any answer to that.

You remember. We said we'd start looking for your mother.

Yes.

For Xmas.

I remember now.

She's always loved silver.

Dad always bought her silver I think.

The candelabra's sensible. It all comes back to you in time.

That's true.

I saw Maureen today.

Maureen Saunderson you mean?

No. Maureen Willis. Wrightson N.M.A.

We haven't seen them for a long time. A long time.

Maureen said that they called in on the McVies when they were on holiday.

How's Colin?

Maureen was very hurt.

She's easily hurt though, Maureen.

Colin hardly spoke. He sat and watched television.

You know Colin. He talks when there is something to say. No small-talk.

He is quiet.

He is a Cassius.

With visitors there though.

Maybe there was a special programme on.

It's only television. And with visitors coming all that way.

I wonder sometimes. Whether the distance makes visitors any more deserving.

Courtesy.

I see that.

It's a courtesy due to visitors.

Courtesy's a great virtue all right. On everybody's part.

Maureen was offended. She won't go back she said. She'd never call again.

Maureen assumes that whenever she calls, people have no greater priority than to listen.

That's cruel.

Selfishness is cruel.

Courtesy may be a sacrifice.

That's true. I can see that point of view.

Real people always deserve more consideration than things; even artistic things.

Is it so though? I say it is, I want to believe it, but am not wholly convinced. Colin has an argument too, I suppose, if he were asked. People have a bland conviction that any company is better than none; and that theirs is preferable to most. They assume that anyone with a book in his hand is killing time; that the person who watches television on his own, is desperate for conversation. There's a good deal of self-opinion in it; and for some, the less reason there is for self-esteem the greater is their presumption of it.

Maybe Colin was watching Jane Austen, or a documentary on lemmings. Few visitors are worth Jane Austen, or a documentary on lemmings in the wild. Mrs Bellis next door is a pleasant woman, and my brother in Napier wouldn't steal a thing, yet they can sit beside me and offer less than Austen on the screen. Their ongoing humanity, the banality of it, is there breathing in and out; kindly eyes, and fingers that close upon the coffee cups. How can the actuality of life, my own above all, compare with the artistic distillation of its essence? Sacrificial art and technology compress things till the glow, otherwise we ride in turn the conversational nags of Unions, investments, conservation, cancer research, and how well the ruas have done; or ilam hardy in your case perhaps. Each of us has a horror that we are as irrelevant to others as we find them to be.

Real people?
What do you mean?
I wondered what were real people.
You've been reading Kafka again, or arguing at work.
I never read Kafka in the summer. Kafka is winter stuff;
season and mood.
Affectation.
Yes, probably so.
Colin didn't care about her.
Or didn't care about her enough, certainly.
She and Brian went all that way, and he barely spoke to them.
Yes.
It's inexcusable.
I suppose it is really.
Maureen said she won't go back.
A punishment, that, on Colin I suppose.
It's your day for sophistry. I've got work to do.

I have too, but it can wait till later. I believe that people are the definition of life: I do, I do. It doesn't pay to admit otherwise. I am close to H. E. Bates; Mr Bellis next door is further from me. We counter each other's neighbourly catch-cries as we pass. The rhetoric of Luther King astounds me from the television, but I fidget by the shelves of jellies and custard powder, while the proprietor warns me of the vandalism outside his shop. Life's dialogue is not in counter-point, and the ironies not pointedly revealed. Art, like a geode within the common stone, amazes with all its colours and its crystals.

I look up too quickly, and catch the view before it's quite assembled, the landscape's face in all its fatiscence; something sardonic and intrinsic is there for an instant at the periphery of vision, like a lizard's tail. Then the trees and breached hills have caught the pose again. Let's say I didn't see it. I didn't see it. As with a Hogarth or a Brueghel print, it doesn't pay to make a close examination.

I'd like to talk to Colin about it all; see again his quirking smile as he listened. Perhaps I should visit him sometime; then again, perhaps not.

The Castle
Of Conceits

There are July days when the sky is inflated by mist to grey immensity, and pearls hang from wires and weather-boards and from the thinnest branches. No wind, and the grey of the sky is milked in the raindrops and in the shallow puddles. Blackbirds forage along the hedges, and foliage is subdued from the frosts of other days. Disconsolate smoke above the suburbs. Posters are cold and calm and stained: they advertise yet another production of Macbeth, and proclaim an evangelical mission long departed. The contagion of the former has overcome the latter: has seeped out and by osmosis reached within the people so that virtue and resolution are undermined. Fruit stares out of place, unwholesome, and in the butchers' shops the meat contracts and beads up blood. Green mould flourishes and marks the seepage on stone walls, and like cigarette paper the birch skin is worn from the boughs. Alley cats shake hands with the invisible, fastidious in the passage from one warehouse to the next. Even the directors' cars, places reserved, are stained and bleed on to the stones embedded in the tar.

Both customers and attendants are present in the shops from duty: each blames the other for the necessity. They despise the product and the prices, the purchaser and the proprietor. Within their common hearing are statements on clothes and thick ankles, walrus moustaches, false jewellery, adam's apples like fists, noses like levelled shotguns, tweed bums that must sidle through the doors. Leached faces, eyes of universal reproach, replicas of smiles of good intent. Barrage balloons of hospitality, politics and the weather are put up to draw the fire. Disillusioned with life, fearful of death; all seek that comfort of gregarious creatures which is the mute realization of shared inconsequence.

A painter's van with the side ladder slips its brakes, runs backwards just a few metres, and shatters the windscreen of the car behind. The event is mundane, but the sound of the glass oddly musical: a chimes which sounds throughout the street. It enters the dreams of Charlotte Ecclestone in her flat above the shop. It is converted into the sound of the hunting horn which gathers shoughs and water-rugs through the heather. Nine people stop to watch: they have their backs to the drift of misty rain. They are made aware by the painter's van that providence is still at work in the world. They may win their golden kiwi yet. They pause to see if there is to be any further spectacle, but only the painter appears. 'Ah, no, Jesus,' he says. The nine people ghost away lest they be approached for help. 'Jesus though. Wouldn't you know it.'

Charlotte expands beneath the purple quilt. As she stretches she draws a vast, prolonged breath as if she has been dead all night, and is come alive again. She lifts her large arms, smooth, and small hands; replaces them beneath the covers for warmth again. Noddy's head marks the ticks, and Big Ears is his companion on the face. Half past twelve and the mist is kissing at the window. 'Why me,' says painter Condell. Charlotte dresses before the heater. Her thighs shimmer as she draws on rugby socks of green and gold; mohair jersey, a skirt of French velvet with a burn covered by a butterfly. She eats the one cold sausage in the fridge, and searches for other items. Dried apricots littered in the cupboard, cracked cheese from which she gnaws out the heart. Her coffee is very hot, and very black. She has a Tam-o-Shanter for her head; winds a varsity scarf around her neck. The ends curl like banded snakes across her bosom. A satchel; a handbag of real and crinkled leather. From the high womb of her coloured flat she descends the dark stairway feet first and despite the danger is born successfully into a grey and milky world in polished brown boots, red velvet with burn and butterfly, and Tam-o-Shanter.

Insubstantial people eddy as froth, indecisive before the crossings, while Charlotte ignores the lights and strides on from block to block.

The leather bag and satchel swing, and diamonds settle on her high cheeks. She stops at Hemmings' delicatessen. Stuffed shoulder and cornish pasties, apple strudel and pin-wheel buns with lemon icing. 'Let the mind feed the mind, and the body feed the body,' she says. The chiropodist beside her nods, and moves aside. Charlotte goes in and waits till Bernie Hemmings can come to serve her. She calculates the distance between the pasties and herself. She positions herself.

'I'm sick of being conned by you, Lottie,' says Bernie Hemmings, but he looks to see that his father is not at the back of the shop, and puts his own back to it. Charlotte takes his hand with icing sugar on the knuckles and places it just under her blouse.

'Go,' she says. It takes Charlotte only a few seconds to put two cornish pasties in a bag: it takes Bernie, dizzy from desire, the same to briefly range one epic breast. Does she ever wear a bra?

'You move fast for a big woman, Lottie,' he says in despair. 'Damn you.' The icing sugar is brushed from his fingers and he imagines it dusted on her curving skin. 'Can I come round tonight?'

'Not tonight.' Bernie watches her leave: red skirt sways from her hips and laps the tops of her polished boots.

'Jesus, Lottie,' says Bernie. His hand is still shaking, and he rests it upon the till to quieten it.

Charlotte sits in 327B and eats her cornish trove. She is early. It is the warmth of the room rather than intellectual impatience which draws her. She finishes her meal, blows up and bursts the bag to startle the three drab and calculating scholars who wait in the rows closer to the front. 'Wordsworth was a simplistic old goat,' she says when the lecturer arrives. 'Wordsworth knew nothing of the life of the people. He wouldn't involve himself in life. Wordsworth has no relevance for modern women.'

'Ah, Miss Ecclestone,' says Dr Taylor wryly, 'last week you rebuked me for Southey, now Wordsworth won't do.'

'Let's have Laurie Lee or Marvell again,' says Charlotte. ' "He hangs in shades the orange bright, like golden lamps in a green night." '

'We are hag-ridden by our prescription.' He admires the presence of Charlotte Ecclestone: the focus of warmth and colour, the generosity of good-natured excess, the challenge to each conventional day. Her shoulders are broad, her hands small, her double chin

seductive; one firm crease and smooth. Wordsworth is both spoken
of and heard with reluctance: thoughts of other things drift like a
vapour. Bursaries and team selections, macaroni cheese and white
upper arms, dying aunts, lost assignments, collapsed pistons, scrutiny
of dreams, chapped lips and visions of apocalypse. Charlotte draws
a picture of Valhalla, and imagines a banquet for all her favourite
poets. She occupies herself with sorting the precedence of seating in
her mind.

'Miss Ecclestone,' says Dr Taylor when people are leaving. 'Miss
Ecclestone.' He holds a finger up in a gesture to delay her. The drab
and calculating scholars of the front rows leave them reluctantly,
wishing the finger was raised for them. Dr Taylor looks at the
bright butterfly on Lottie's red skirt, and her magnificent chest.
'I was disappointed to find that as yet you have made no entry for
the Slye poetry award. It closes on the seventeenth, you see.'

'I've been so busy. The hurly-burly.'

'As long as you're aware of it. So few have bothered for the right
reasons.'

'I might start something tonight. There's been the play and
everything.'

'There's still time,' the lecturer says. He watches her go, and
decides uncritically that Wordsworth should be deleted from the
prescription. 'There's still time,' he says.

Charlotte leaves the campus. A foggy cloud hangs on the buildings,
and a fug within the library. She boards a bus in Crosse Street, and
finds she knows the driver by sight. They smile at each other in
defiance of the weather and all probabilities. Each time the bus
stops and starts he smiles at her. Charlotte likes the agile, decisive
way he moves: she likes the strong tendons in the back of his hand:
she likes the contrast of his watch strap on the brown skin and hair
of his wrist. She likes his square, neat sideburns. 'Have you ever
thought of varying your route?' she says.

'People depend on a set time-table you see. It's laid down.'

'Too much,' says Charlotte. 'But towards the end of a run most
people are getting off aren't they?'

'Pretty much.'

'At the end of a run you could go on a few blocks. I mean you
are the captain of the ship.'

'Sometimes if the roads are dangerous or that, I'll make a detour, make changes.'

'I'm only a few blocks further on. I thought you might like to come on up.'

'I've got other runs,' he says. 'I could ring in sick I suppose.' His eyes start to jiggle. Charlotte breathes in deeply, and her breast rises like a spinnaker.

'No time or thought for all that,' she says. 'Come now or not at all. Act on impulse or not at all. To commit yourself to a moment is a pledge of its value.' Murray sees the small knuckles of her hand, the mist which glints on her dark hair, her cheeks, her Tam-o-Shanter. 'Ostler Street,' she says.

Murray swings the bus to a halt, and vaults out of his seat. He hurries down the bus to the last two old ladies; one green, one blue. 'You'll have to get out here,' he says. 'The brakes have gone. We could start rolling back any minute. I can't take the risk of going on.' He gallantly carries their baskets down the steps, and urges them into the drizzle. The green lady is the smaller; she has a bad leg. Murray takes her arm for a few metres till she settles into a rhythm. 'There you are,' he says. 'On your way.' The bus begins again; swiftly hissing along the wet streets.

'I am the captain of my ship,' says Murray with the conviction of sudden decision. 'We won't leave it by the shops, but there's that little dead-end street by the lodge. Rice Street. We'll whip it in there and no-one will be any the wiser.' Murray drives the bus into Rice Street, to the very end, and leaves the blunt nose of the bus jutting over the steps of the lodge.

'Bring plenty of money,' says Charlotte. 'You don't want to have to come back for it.' Murray takes a fist of notes, and a palm of silver as though it were only gravel.

'Jesus,' he says. 'Hardly anyone needs a bus at this time of day anyway. In this weather they're better off inside. They're nearly all old people wanting library books and lambskins for their beds.' He comes and stands beside Charlotte. As a test of her sincerity he intends to give a horse-bite above the left knee, but the circumference of flesh is such that it becomes merely a pinch. Charlotte smiles at him. She closes her eyes for a moment as she smiles, and her long lashes lie down upon her cheeks.

'Let the mind feed the mind, and the body feed the body,' she says.

'That's right,' says Murray.

He doesn't look back at the bus as they leave it. He turns up the collar of his jacket, the way he has seen hard cases do in the films, and he blesses what he regards as providence. 'This was such a foul day too,' he says.

'Do you like camembert cheese?' Charlotte says.

'Do I.' He is captive to the contrast of black curls on her ears.

'Buy three tins,' she says. 'And oysters. You like fried oysters?'

'A-Ah.' The tasselled ends of her scarf flutter. Murray straightens his back to ensure that in her boots she is no taller than he as they walk.

'And a bottle of Barsac,' says Charlotte. 'You've got enough money for Barsac?' Murray has no idea, but he can see the red velvet skirt swirling from her hips like a flame amidst the mist. He holds up the bunched notes from his pocket. 'Two bottles of Barsac would be better,' she says. 'And hot bread perhaps.' Murray sees her small hands; the nails delicate. There is nothing gross in Charlotte. Physical size and power are more than balanced by dimension of the spirit.

Murray allows her to choose the shops and purchases. In her aura the corruption of the grey day is powerless. The world in water-colour wash is just a backdrop and the canvas trembles. 'Did you see me in Macbeth?' says Charlotte. 'I was Lady Macduff, but I wanted to be Lady Macbeth. Come to that I wanted to be Macbeth.' They rise up the stairs to her rooms, carrying the things that they will share.

Charlotte lights the open fire. Dry, flared pine cones serve for kindling. 'I love fires,' she says. 'I'd like to be an arsonist; set things ablaze. Huge things, irreplaceable things, precious things, all going up with a roar. Such a moment must give a sense of grandeur and fearsomeness to life. To stand transfixed and see a parable of flames.' Murray watches the writhing of the pine cones; the petals incandescent.

'Children understand fire,' he says.

'Fire is eternal catharsis. Fire is the act of substance giving up its essence.' Charlotte pushes the table closer to the heat, and sets out the oysters, bread, wine, and the round cheeses. Her light shade is of hand-crafted coloured glass that casts additional colours to those of the fire. Murray is pale blue, and Charlotte oriental. The oysters in their batter are chameleon to no avail between the plate and mouth.

'This is the life,' says Murray. He takes a swallow of Barsac, cautiously, then another with wondering contentment.

'It's not much of a day for driving.'

'It could be worse. It could be ice, you see. That's when it's tricky for a bus in this city. But there's satisfaction. The bus can be a world too, distinct from everything outside.'

'A technological denial of what is imposed. There are many ways to defeat the appearance of things. But driving buses on a set route: it must be the miniature golf of transport.'

It is not often that anyone bothers to talk to Murray about his job. He eats the last oyster, and drinks more Barsac to provide it habitat. 'It's other people though, isn't it,' he says. 'And they don't think of the driver after a time you know. Just part of the bus and disregarded. I like to watch their faces as they look down through the windows at other people. All their life is in their faces. They can't help it. They lose their own masks as they watch people who are unaware they're being watched.'

'A series of emotional reflections.'

'Yes.'

'A waitress or a lift operator must have a wonderful sense of species,' Charlotte says. She puts three more cones on the fire and balances a chunk of bright coal with absorbed deliberation. 'I only burn anthracite if I can, because of the appearance, the gleam of it you see.' The gem coal leaves barely a smudge on her fingers. 'Have you any pain?' she says.

'No.'

'Neither have I. Have you any serious regrets; any grand hopes and promises; anything of awesome threat or significant demarcation?' Murray smiles: such conversation must represent humour. Antipodean reticence should be discarded for no other reason.

'I feel great,' he says.

'It's just that I take stock occasionally: snap the shutter sometimes on my life to frame assessments. The world is spinning fiercely while we are here. Here not there, this time not another. Immense concentration is needed to maintain actuality.' The anthracite falls silently in two, and new flames appear. 'And we have no pain. You said you feel great.'

Murray draws his hand across the bright velvet of her skirt. 'All the colours of this room,' he says. 'I don't know how you do it. That glass lamp is something.' Charlotte lifts her hand before the facets of the table lamp. Her skin changes colour.

'It is my castle of conceits.' She undulates her arms to catch the light. Murray pushes her skirt up and lets his hand trace her nearer thigh. The circumference, the passage of his hand, seem to go on for ever. 'E. E. Cummings said break up the white light of objective realism into the secret glories which it contains.'

'This is the place for that all right,' says Murray. Charlotte looks at the remaining food.

'God, this stuff,' she says. 'I'll blow right up on this food. Fatter and fatter.' She takes off her skirt: one knee is caught in a faint lilac bruise from the lamp. She admires Murray's clean hair, and the straight hair of his chest narrowing to a dark line down his belly; and his ribs showing like straps below the muscles of his side. 'I don't know how men keep the fat off,' she says.

'Metabolism,' says Murray vaguely, and then more forcefully. 'It's the jogging. I run for thirty minutes most nights.'

'I tried it once,' she says. 'I tried it, but I couldn't think as I ran. The effort kept breaking in on my thoughts, so I gave it up.'

'Ah,' says Murray. His head has ended too close to the fire, and the thick hair is in danger of being set alight. All of him is being set alight. The anthracite coal gleams of itself black, and in the varied flames of its essence, and the crafted glass lamp gives changing colours to movement: kaleidoscope of sex, and the Barsac in the bottle as strong a colour as a ginger cat.

Murray's trousers have become rolled inside out, and one sock lost down a leg. Charlotte watches him sorting it out. He stops to say, 'I've just thought about the bus still parked there in Rice Street. Parked there outside the lodge, hours ago, and no word to the depot when I didn't come back.'

'What will you say?' The manipulation of phenomena is always of interest to her.

'I'll think of something.'

'Of course you will.'

'It would have worried me to plan in advance, but I feel I'll have no trouble at all in thinking of something. A dozen things could have happened.'

'More,' says Charlotte. 'Each moment has infinite possibility of development.'

'Anyway, I've a good record there and there'll be no bother. Any story will be swallowed once.'

'Of course it will. One oddity will remind them of your reliability,' Charlotte says, 'and let me know how it works out.'

'Oh I'll be back to tell you all about it.' He puts on his jacket, and kisses her.

'Saturday's a good day,' she says. 'I'd come down, but I can't be bothered getting dressed again.'

'Saturday,' says Murray. He grins and goes quickly down the stairs: he draws his chin into his jacket in expectation of experience beyond Charlotte's flat.

Rain has come with the night, and the mist which has reconnoitred all the city is reinforced by the main body. The southerly hurries the rain in; driving it around corners, down alleys, into soft, rotten crevices and bubbling through cracks against gravity. The streets are cold and slick, milky and cold. Gutter water begins its proletarian song, and shadows like acrobats swing and twist independent from the wires and cars and neons that cause them. And the rain has shadows as Murray goes, dark fans behind the squalls like a howlet's wing.

Charlotte runs a bath and watches the steam billow out into the other rooms, and twist before her fire and table lamp. She will begin her poem for the Slye award. All the world for her is shrunk to three rooms, and will expand again within her mind.

The Visualiser

'There's something about real leather I say,' said Wattie. He bounced a moment in the bucket seat; his heavy, lined face wore a judicious expression as he tested the comfort. 'Ah, yes,' he said and leant back a little to ease the passage of a belch which filled the car with the reek of chicken pieces and beer.

'Sorry about that.'

'For Christ's sake.'

'Get a fair bit of indigestion now actually,' said Wattie in an aggrieved voice and he bared his mare's teeth in a yawn.

Angus felt the familiar pleasure when he crossed the overhead bridge and turned off the motorway, leaving the city behind. The Rover sped away from the Friday traffic into the indeterminate area of mismanaged fields and professional homes. Wattie's came before his own. 'Come in and have a drink,' said Wattie eagerly, as he struggled to get out of the car, seeming to wish to get both arms and legs out first and so leaving his carcass rolling awkwardly.

Angus told him that he wouldn't bother. 'As a matter of fact it's my birthday.' Wattie thought that all the more reason for going in, but Angus shook his head, waved and went on. Within six miles he reached his own place and turned up the short, gravel path through the shrubs. The grounds which Wattie and the land agent had been so adamant were a necessity; must have a house with 'grounds' had been Wattie's sole instinct for the occasion.

After dinner he joked about it with Lillian; both enjoying their mild mockery of the head of the firm. Angus smoked the pipe that Bruce had given him for his birthday. A sour, varnished thing without a proper filter. 'An excellent pipe,' he told Bruce when his son reluctantly left the television set and went to bed. For a time Angus watched Lillian ironing and then he took what was left of the Saint-Emilion claret into his study and drank it there, while going over his audit figures for northern Aluminium Pressings. When he went upstairs Lillian was sitting in bed with a pad on her knees, writing to her mother. 'Tell her I had a good birthday,' said Angus, 'and thank her for the shirts. I hope the necks are big enough this time.'

'They could be changed anyway.'

'Yes I suppose so.'

Lillian finished the letter and began to talk about the antique sideboard that Alice Getheren had bought, but when Angus sighed in boredom she broke off with a laugh to put her hands affectionately on his shoulder. 'Happy birthday hero,' she said.

For a time after she was asleep Angus lay awake. His stomach was a bit off and he wondered if he had overdone the wine. Twice when he was almost asleep he thought of points concerning his work and reached out quietly to make jottings on the pad by his bed.

Later in the night he had the dream of the Krools. The cold was like nothing he had ever experienced before; a cold so intense it was a total almost unendurable ache, and the desolate surface without horizon was crystal clear in the bright, plum-purple light.

He felt himself rocking sluggishly in the heavy gases of his case as a Krool checked the lead from his primal sonic eye and gave him further injections at the scale junctures. The agony of cold seemed to abate slightly and in the crystal light he could see a myriad oscillating protein orbs, staring stupidly with their inbred eyes. Lesser Krools moved effortlessly amongst them; finding the ripe ones, snapping their thermal stalks and letting them drift in the magnetic field towards the cargo points, some still and lop-sided, others flexing convulsively and with a little purple gas seeping from their anal baffles.

The Krool rotated him once more for a final check and said, 'I think he's right now. I've gone up in the dosage a bit, but no more than warranted. Happy birthday hero! Now that is good. You've got to hand it to this one, no wonder the orbs do better than ever before; happy birthday Angus!' The other Krools took the message and raised their muzzles, breaking the silence of the purple sky with their laughter; a bitter, depreciatory sound which gradually became Bruce's shouts and the excited barking of Prospero as he was released from his chain.

Angus could see about him the irrefutable and trivial evidence of reality. His left shoe with three crease lines across the instep; the stain not far away on the carpet where Bruce had spilt coffee four years before; the bruise on the lip of the mahogany duchess where he had dropped his electric razor while shaving. Even the familiar smell of his own forearm on which his head lay was comforting.

Yet it wasn't until mid-morning that he mentioned the dream to Lillian, not because of any reaction she might have, but because it took him that long to reduce it in his mind to the point at which he could recount it lightly, as he felt it must be recounted. 'It sounds awful Angus. What a funny thing. It's not like you to have dreams like that.' Angus described the floating protein orbs, simulating what he imagined to be a look of oafish bewilderment, and they laughed together, secure in their harmony. As he went back out to finish the lawn however Angus returned briefly to the topic.

'So bloody cold and bare though. And that odd purple brightness,' he said quietly. 'I hope that's the last of it.'

It wasn't the last of it, although for two months it seemed to be. Angus stopped thinking about the dream, but it never faded from his mind. It was like a vivid scar upon the body; known in detail, but not examined any more. In August he and Wattie went up to Tunidge for an important audit on the books of Roscoe's the plastics manufacturer. They had a room in the new Motor Inn and on the second night Angus met the Krools again. When the cold began to come, he knew, and he tried to retreat to wakefulness, to wreck his own credulity and so escape. It's a dream, a bloody dream, only a dream he told himself, but the cold gripped him in an agony until he thought his head would split like a frosted plum, and the purple crystal of the light again revealed that simple desolation: the orbs in haphazard stages of development, rank on rank of them about him, jogging a little like filled bladders as they heeled before the space wind, and even the vivid sheen of the Krools was blanched almost white by the cold.

One was treating Angus in his case again; more injections and the scrutiny of trailing jacks. 'I think Angus is conscious.' The Krool had a sullen tone and gave way quickly to a much larger Krool which reared up beside it, the great purple crest afire.

'This is the second lapse. You know how unfavourably the growth rate of the orbs reflects any disturbance of the therapeutic visualiser and more important, any loss of confidence in his therapeutic reality could destroy the usefulness of Angus entirely.' Almost tenderly the Krool rotated Angus.

'It's the occasional pulsing in drug use of this one,' complained the lesser Krool. 'Makes it very hard to calculate the hallucinatory doses.'

The crested Krool ignored the remark and holding the base of one of Angus's filter lobes to assess the gaseous exchange, he carried out the remaining injections himself. As Angus became warmer the Krool relaxed a little. 'Do you realize how scarce these things are now in the three galaxies?' he asked the still subdued lesser Krool. 'Do you want to spend your life finding and caring for the orbs in the old way?' Before Angus left them he could see on the periphery of his vision a particularly pale Krool caught between two of the largest orbs as he attempted to harvest one. The Krool's reptilian body arched only once and ineffectively against the aimless immensity of the orbs and then ceased to struggle and began to drift with the things it had killed towards the holding points.

Wattie was standing between their beds when Angus awoke, peering into the hotel mirror, ruefully rolling the fat of his stomach between the thumb and forefinger of his free hand. He saw Angus was awake and his face expanded into customary good-humour. 'Morning Angus. Got to keep moving you know. Lloyd will be picking us up at eight.'

'Morning Wattie.' My god, said Angus to himself, dear bloody god. He rolled his head in desperation as if to rid himself of the Krools.

'. . . Although the big one seemed to me to be ready for any approach. Freddy Gredgelaw told me that all the waitresses in these new expensive places are up to it. Big tits. You can say what you like Angus, there's something about big tits. It's just as well we're married and that, cause the big tits on that dark one . . .'

Angus nodded absently. Dear bloody god he thought, close to tears. There's something wrong. Inside him was the seed of the conviction that the world of the Krools was more than some random nightmare sequence. As he dressed he fought for self-control and while they breakfasted and Wattie nudged him when the dark one with the big tits served them, Angus could see still in his mind's eye the alert head and swaying crest of the great Krool.

Tunidge marked a watershed for Angus; after it he was never able to disregard the Krools again. It was a symptom of his concern that he said nothing of the second dream to Lillian and in the week after his return he kept an appointment with Maurice Smith the specialist. Besides being a notable short iron player Smith was well thought of as a psychiatrist by the medical profession.

He laughed easily when Angus joked about the absence of a couch and a notebook, and while Angus told him about the Krools he listened quietly, saying 'Goodness,' from time to time and smoothing the soft hair of his sideboards. He said Angus's dream was the best he had heard for a long time and seemed quite interested. 'What do you think it represents?' he asked Angus ingenuously.

'They're not like any other dreams I've had,' began Angus defensively. 'They have a disturbing conviction. It sounds foolish, but the reason they worry me is mostly the implication that the dream is reality and reality a dream. The second time there was the suggestion that what I experience is fed back to the orbs as some sort of conditioning to keep them placid and well growing.'

'Like music for cows?' said Smith brightly.

'The therapeutic visualiser the Krools called it. One of the things that's so disconcerting is that I seem to know a lot about the orbs and so on when I see them, and names too. How do I know what the Krools are called when the name is never mentioned in the dream?'

'Quite. Quite so.' Smith nodded, almost it seemed in wonder.

'I noticed one thing though,' said Angus, eager for reassurance. 'At the end of the first time the noise of the Krools sort of merged with the sound of our dog as I woke, how dreams do sometimes. Thinking about it afterwards I thought this was proof that Prospero's barking before I was awake had been used by my mind as the Krool's sound, and therefore the thing must have been imagination.'

Smith leant forward intently, as if he were about to demonstrate the use of the pitching wedge to carry the bunker yet hold the green. 'Logically of course, Angus, that's not really proof. You see in fact the barking of the Krools could have been utilized by your sub-conscious in creating the sound of Prospero, rather than vice-versa. I'm not trying to damage your confidence, just establish a pattern of clear thinking.'

'Yes, I see that.' Angus nevertheless felt regret at the passing of one further small consolation.

'You see Angus, reason must be the touchstone and reason only. It's all we have. I'm not treating you as a patient in the normal way, because I don't think you are one. Our acquaintance over the last few years has been slight, but I know you better than you might think. You've had these unusually vivid and cogent dreams because yours is an unusually vivid and cogent mind. Accept them for what they are: a release from everyday pressures.'

'It's just I'd like some way to satisfy myself that's all they are.'

'No. Don't go looking for any tricks. Just weigh the solidity and intricacy of the life you know against the vision of yourself as something apparently permanently hallucinating for the benefit of these Krools, eh?'

'I guess so.'

'After all we are all in a classic Bishop Berkeley situation really you know.'

Smith accompanied Angus towards the door, his arm draped in comradely dismissal upon Angus's shoulders. As he turned back into his office Smith assumed a crouching stance and cocked his wrists for the pretence of a controlled, lofted shot with an eight iron.

The visit failed to put Angus at ease; it proved nothing and deep within himself Angus repressed the apprehension that Smith himself was just a figment of his own irrepressible creation. He found that he was still searching for ways to settle the matter. It came to him three days later, as he was dictating to Susanne and he felt only a tightening of the chest and a coppery taste at the back of his throat. 'Sleep, night time,' he said calmly, and Susanne giggled and tugged at the hem of her dress. Smith had said let reason be the touchstone and so he did. Susanne looked at his still face and started to talk, but Angus told her that he would finish the dictation later and she went out.

The more he thought objectively about the idea of sleep, the more he was convinced that he had found the way; the over-lap, the tunnel between the world of the Krools and the world of Lillian, Wattie and floribunda roses. Angus saw clearly then that sleep was really just the time when contact was made, and that because he slept so he created in reassuring variety and specious reasonableness 'sleep' for other organisms of his world. Sleep was in fact the return to the Krools, though only twice had he been aware of it; and fatigue was the need for the medicine of the Krools to keep his world fresh about him. Angus felt both satisfaction and fear; satisfaction that he had at last a means of putting the Krools to the test, and fear at what might be the consequence of it.

Almost light-heartedly he called Susanne in again and finished the letter explaining the application of retrospective customs duties to his client's case. His conscientiousness in the circumstances gave him an odd feeling, like a last irrelevant lesson in the upper school with the place to the university already won. Angus went through into Wattie's office to tell him that he would be taking a long week-end and he felt an oddly poignant fondness for the companionable decency of his partner. Wattie crouched determinedly at his desk, his lips shaping some of the words as he read, belying the shrewdness of his understanding. Angus's request seemed to fill him with regret that he had not thought of it himself. 'Hell Angus, you go ahead. Both of us are getting too chained to this office. We'll find some convention or something next month in our own field too, and go away to it and have a blow-out.'

At the door Angus paused. 'Ever wondered if life is real, Wattie?' he said. Wattie was puzzled and looked up at Angus for his cue, his Biro poised above the papers. Angus felt suddenly foolish, so laughed and said, 'You know. Outside, Wattie: the world we read about, Kruger National Park, the South Seas, Santiago, Timbuctoo.'

'Oh yeah.' Wattie's face cleared. 'Like that joke, ah, something about the resurrection, ah, or something and it ends up with Call This Living!' Wattie laughed heartily at the inconclusive punch-line of a joke he couldn't recall and Angus laughed too.

He stayed awake all that night by finishing work for Wattie and when he told Lillian he wanted a few days at the river by himself she seemed to understand. On the Friday he drove up there, turning through the yellow-blossomed gorse and bumping over the stones of the track before he reached the crib. It was so quiet that the air seemed to be faintly ringing and after unpacking the car he sat in his corduroy trousers on the sagging verandah and let the sun shine full on his face. The warmth loaded his arms and legs until movement was difficult and his head lolled against the wooden verandah support, but he kept himself from falling asleep by getting up unsteadily and taking his rod off to the river.

As he stood in his waders at the head of the Turk pool which he had fished so often and looked up over the cress, rushes and gravel stretches of the river bed, towards the scrubby hills with their poor, clay soils, he found it hard to take the Krools seriously and easy to suppose that overwork, or some such, was all he had to contend with. The fabric of his familiar world contained too much detailing and wonder to be his own creation; yet there was a sense of brittleness since the Krools had been revealed to him and Angus knew that he wouldn't sleep until he had proved the thing one way or the other.

That night he had to keep moving about to stay awake; walking up and down the dim verandah and even seeing if he could crawl through the table legs without brushing them. When at last the day came, he felt better for a time and he was making a drink of coffee when Cedric from the store pedalled down to the crib.

'Saw the Rover go past,' he said. 'Been delivering stuff to Nigel Oakes who's in the Pullinew place for a few days. I thought you might need something and it would save you coming up. I'm going past each day see.'

'I brought up all I'll need I think, Cedric. I'm only up for the weekend rest really. Thanks though.'

'Fine. You look a bit seedy actually. You'll come right up here.'

'That's right.'

Angus had thought, for no particular reason, that if he forced the return to the Krools it would come at night, but as Cedric pedalled back up the track with the empty cane basket bouncing from the handle-bars, the first distortion formed. The broom and gorse to Cedric's left wilted and for an instant became the tightly clustered, purple coils of the vegetation of Epsilon Sadducee in the second galaxy. And the line of the morning sun on the slopes to the west of the river faltered as he heard the dry rustle of the space wind. The images reassembled, but Angus knew that the test was on: he resisted the almost overwhelming fatigue and stood there on the quiet verandah, his hands clenched and the forgotten kettle hissing steam in the room behind him.

The resolution of the true images came partially, like the stripping of old wall-paper; so to the right of his vision the sky and half the land were gone and in their place the spreading, purple crystal light, the protein orbs, the docks, the reaching cold of the space wind which seemed to freeze the tears on his cheeks. 'Oh Jesus, it's all true,' mumbled Angus, and hopelessness filled him up, as his hills and his sky and the Turk pool, all ran in a state of flux as a painted mask.

Many Krools were gathered about him. 'Angus is fully conscious now,' said one. 'There's no doubt he intentionally resisted the service coma, and realizes what is the truth.' With brilliant, azure eyes beneath his crest, the great Krool came and gazed down at Angus.

'The orbs won't idle for harvest without a visualiser, Angus, and you have too much resistance now.' The Krool took hold of Angus firmly. 'I'll disconnect all the leads at once,' he said, choosing to speak inaudibly.

'Thank you,' replied Angus. The cold spread through him very quickly. He felt his scales lift feebly in response to some atavistic muscular response, and his filter lobes were soon unable to continue gaseous exchange. 'I wish I may have died home on Phi Romana.'

'It's better this way,' said the great Krool, not altogether unkindly. 'There aren't any of you left on Phi Romana.'

Another
Generation

The patio illumine was the single source of light; diffused through glass, influenced in progress by the colours, textures, shapes of furniture and ornaments until the room was dim hued, an aquarium, and movement met resistance from the liquid air. Lucretia was curled in a corner of the large sofa, and Franc urged his claim. His fingers trailed over her left heel, and he traced the relaxed achilles tendon of her ankle. Please. His voice was thickened by anticipation and aquarium air. You can trust yourself with me. Please. The flesh of his neck had a slight sheen of sweat, attractive in the intimacy of that partial light. We need to, he said. What sort of balance have you got? A hundred, two hundred thousand, both earned and given. Tell me how you keep your money. Tell me all the things you do with it; the ways you calculate the interest; all the forms of investment and return you've found. Tell me again those strange things you do with silver.

Lucretia breathed heavily although at rest; as a pouting fish breathes in conscious satisfaction of life sustained. The ruffles of her blouse flared like gills, and were caught in ripples of merging green light, green shadow, as they moved. She looked through the full length windows and glass doors to the patio; saw above the mask of garden trees a dusted pattern of stars. You could give me silver coins, said Franc. His fingers continued a play of stops along her heel. It's a thing with you — pure silver coins. You could lay out hundreds in the moonlight, white mounds all pressing down. If you trusted me; if you loved me.

I can't, said Lucretia. As he said silver coins her mouth had opened and eyelids drooped for an instant, but her face was turned away.

Please.

I can't yet, but soon; when we're sure of each other. You know I love you.

How do I know. I don't know, said Franc. His whisper was harsh and close. Lucretia began to weep. Let me give you used notes: he used a lover's voice. All worn notes; warm and worn, the corners frayed like the toes of old slippers, the colours darkened by the alchemy of a thousand palms and purposes. Some have things written on them — names, phone numbers, shopping lists, poetry. They're so old and knowing, like tobacco leaves, with veins of their own life beginning to form again; but old notes are from a tree more ancient even, and with a more persistent fragrance. Used notes at the last are cynical, pleasured, corrupt with all the venal impulse to which they must submit.

Don't, don't, Lucretia murmured.

Please. Just a straight missionary gift then?

I can't: not yet.

Marx, said Franc, jerking his head. He sat up abruptly and began to put on his shoes. Lucretia sobbed beside him. It was a familiar ending between them. A lace snapped because of his impatience, and he swore again — Ricardo. He next spoke calmly, with an effort, ashamed that Lucretia was weeping. I'm sorry. I don't want to upset you, you know that.

We could have sex, she said: an offer of reconciliation.

We can have that anytime, with anyone. It means nothing. A vacant, instinctual rabbiting.

I love you. I want to share the most intense of emotions with you. Franc was eager for agreement, but she was downcast at the injustice yet necessity of her caution. Franc stood in the blurred shadows to put on his jacket. He stroked Lucretia's head; ran one blouse ruffle between thumb and finger to assure her of affection. I've got to go, he said. It's all right. Forget it. I'll ring you tomorrow.

Lucretia's parents were also concerned for her. They talked of it when she had gone upstairs to her room. Her eyes are red; she's been crying, Mrs Rand said.

What is the matter with her these days? Mr Rand's voice was vigorous with worry and impatience. Why does she keep on with him if they can't be happy. I'm Benthamed if I know.

I think Franc's too serious, and she doesn't want to commit herself.

They're not financing each other are they?

Sol!

Well, I don't understand young people these days. Money is all they think about. And there's no bounds of decency or restraint any more you know. They even hang around the banks and share rooms and make suggestions to people coming in and out. It all needs cleaning up. They caress money in full view in the parks, and whistle at the millionaires. Kids miss school to go gambling together, or sniffing mint dyes.

They're just more open about it, I suppose, and you know Franc's quite brilliant at his job. He's on 100,000 a year, and in three super and pension groups. Lucretia says he's seven major forms of security asset, and not all in this country.

I know, yes, I know, said Mr Rand, but it's all so calculating and deliberate now isn't it. So selfish. You and I weren't always moneying when we first married. We didn't talk about it much; we kept our feelings in check. Look at television and video news now; all details of mergers, frauds, extortion; robbery cases and close-ups of the tellers' faces after they've passed over all the money, and interviews with lottery winners and bankrupts before they've a chance to control their emotions. Drooling coverage of self-immolation; people swallowing the new doubloon which precisely blocks the windpipe. It's disgusting. And the Unions with reports of non-existent wage rounds every month to keep the workers titillated. It debases everything; it does. I'm serious.

It's that financial lodge of yours.

No, I'm serious. From the necessary economic motivation and medium of exchange, money's perverted to a personal buzz. No-one remembers its social purpose any more.

Stop worrying, and come to bed. Things change.

I mean it. It's a worrying thing that's happening, said Mr Rand. Where it leads and so on.

Come to bed and I'll tell you how the old man Henessey made all his money, and what he does with it.

You don't know.

I do though.

Aw, come on now, said Mr Rand.

I do though. Mabel Henessey got excited at our share club and told me it all. You wouldn't believe about old man Henessey, and he looks so righteous. I know for sure that sometimes he - - -. Even though they were alone, Mrs Rand leant ladylike to her husband's ear to impart her story.

Is that a fact, said Mr Rand. Well I'll be Keynesed.

Franc drove late at night from the residential heights of the Rands, to the entertainment section of the city strung along John Stuart Mill Boulevard and Laski Street. All that time with Lucretia in the muted light; the affection, the stalemate. He was still breathing deeply, and he could feel the pulse beat at the sides of his neck. He idled down Laski Street in the indulgence district; one more cruising electric car in a line of them, between the loan shops, parlours, coin halls, speciality stands and dough flick cinemas. Franc parked outside one of the smaller arcades. He rested there; telling himself that he needed the rest, and perhaps might do no more than that. He thought of Lucretia; how her breathing became when she was talking of solid silver; how she was in thrall to the cool, moon metal and would place her tongue between her teeth and gently bite when she saw such coins. He thought of his own father, and what he was making day after day after day. Franc knew his father was behind Pan Globe Enterprises, and that he personally gave bonuses to fifty-three executives; one by one in his office each year.

From his car, Franc could see the display of titles in the speciality video shop; hot sellers of the moment. Borrowers and Lenders Be, Mortgage Mistress, What's In Kitty, The Buck Stops Here, and the notorious Cash Me In. He took his thick wallet from the dash locker, and left the car. He was deliberate, yet there was a sense of disappointment in himself within his deliberate mood. Franc ignored the appraising faces of the groups along the arcade frontage. To stand was to suggest interest, and he kept walking, kept his eyes glancing past the faces, until he reached the bankcard vending machines deep in the arcade. The police had grown weary of moving people on; graffiti blossomed on the walls and were interpolated into the intructions themselves; reefs of champagne cans had been built up by the wall and capped with plastic spoons from Jumbo pies. Yet the noise, the movement, the colour and the commerce, kept all tense and defiant.

Like a favourite coral terrace in the reef, the vending wall had its special shoal, its own population; constant, yet ever changing in its pattern; intimate only within itself, yet ever conscious of others watching; twisting out from the vending machines with smiles and body language to be observed, then circling back in to recapture conversation and resume a pose. Franc watched a chunky young man with a Roman fringe. The young man had a gold coin in his hand which was always moving. In obsessive ritual it appeared between each pair of fingers in turn, dipped into the palm, scudded against gravity like a modest, yellow mouse across the back of his hand. Goldy circled out twice from the wall, then came a third time, stood by Franc and performed his easy actions with the coin. He smiled with closed lips to himself, as though he considered Franc was about to say something both humorous and predictable. I want you to give me used notes, said Franc.

Whatever you say, squire. I've a place handy.

I haven't time, said Franc. Just come further into the arcade.

Whatever suits your fancy, squire, said Goldy.

In a recessed doorway to the closed office of an investment counsellor, Franc gave up his thick wallet, and leant his shoulder into the corner to give him support against the onslaught of ecstasy. Goldy ran notes over Franc's face and hands, crinkled them tenderly beside his ear, insinuated them into the slits of his shirt front. Worn, used notes frayed and soiled to the texture of skin; worn as skin, natural as skin, necessary as skin and sin, scented with usury and compromises and enslavements and desires. Tokens of power, each with its colours of face value a dim nationality in the recess of the doorway.

Goldy was at once skilful and contemptuous, and all the time his own gold remained in his hand, rustling mouse-like amongst the paper money. Goldy took the sweat from Franc's forehead with notes as soft napkins. This is your thing all right, squire, he said. Franc buckled in the corner, breathing as if stabbed.

Talk to me; talk to me, he said. The notes were familiar, like sections of worn sheets; finely creased and tinged with inflicted experience. Goldy gripped some notes and imposed tension until they tore with the sound of a small fire crackling in its grate. Tens were royal blue, twenties rust orange, and others green and yellow: all colours rendered subtle by usage, and barely more than degrees of shadow in the doorway where Goldy and Franc were close together. I said talk to me, said Franc.

Baht, rupee, escudo, chon, the obedient whisper began. Centavos, peso, florins, centime, rial, colon, satung, piaster, lek, schilling, lira, stater, drachma, krona. Some notes crumpled and fell, lay amongst their feet on the tiled floor of the investment counsellor's small portico. Dinars, talents, zloty, aurei, quetzal, crowns, gulden, cedi, shekel, yen, groschen, ruble. Franc's eyes rolled. The white of them caught light from the arcade of indulgences and was tinged with green-blue like the white of a hard boiled egg. There we are then, squire. The two of them were close together in the deep doorway, and notes like worn tongues, with all the knowing and unknowing language, passed between them.

People in search of mercenary pleasure came back and forth in the arcade. The automatic vending machines clicked obligingly, car horns and insolent cries echoed from the street, a youth sprayed dollar signs and kissed them dry, and the neons in the arcade glowed as living coral in tropical intensity. Opposite Franc's doorway a message in pink incessantly began on the left and ran off to the right again, again. Money Is The Best Charge, it said.

At
The Door

'They're quite strict about it here aren't they?'

'It's only a few minutes now.'

'In Blenheim I was allowed in almost any time to see him; except after ten. I used to stay during meals often. They had very good meals in Blenheim.'

'Perhaps here where they're all on specialist's care they have to be more strict. And there's the size of the place; big places are more formal aren't they.'

'Only I haven't a lot of time this afternoon. My daughter comes over from Lyttelton Fridays to the keep fit classes, and I go back with her at four.'

'I think it's only a minute or two now. I think I saw the sister walking through to check.'

'She likes herself a bit I find, that sister.'

'They get used to the authority.'

'It's all taxpayers' money though isn't it. I think a lot of these people forget it's all taxpayers' money.'

'Yes.'

'He got drained on Monday.'

'Yes, they drained him on the Monday, and he could hardly talk when I saw him. It's as if they drained too much I thought. His face seemed all scraped away from the inside.'

'Here is a nurse.'

'No. She's just on the way through to the linen room. They don't like to meet your eyes do they. Ever notice that? I've been in the linen room, and they keep it very nice actually. I don't think you can fault the hygiene in our hospitals. In Blenheim it was the same, only a lot smaller of course, but the same hygiene I mean.'

'I think we're lucky in this country.'

'And your man's in here.'

'Yes, almost a week now.'

'He's been in five months mine has. And before that three and a half months in Blenheim. He won't come out you know. He knows he won't come out. After they drained him on Monday I think he knew it. All the time I was with him that afternoon he kept holding my hand, and tried to talk about the past, only he found it hard to talk. Remember this and remember that it was, and he's never been one to talk much about the past before. He's always let bygones be bygones. Let bygones be bygones he'd always say. He kept pressing my hand at the thought of things. Things in the past.'

'He's having a low time perhaps.'

'I rung the doctor that night because I couldn't find him after visiting. He was very nice, very agreeable about it. Posited terminal was one of the things he said, and likely to succumb. They mean he won't come out you see.'

'I'm sorry.'

'It's not easy though is it. No matter what sort of life you've had, it's not easy. And on Wednesday he was the same you know, only he could talk about it better. He talked about the children when they were babies and that. He remembered things I never even thought he knew. Their toys and that. They've children of their own now. He remembered Susan put Winnie the Pooh in the bath, and afterwards she cried when the sound thing inside rusted and a stain came through on the outside. I'd forgotten it myself.'

'With all the time to fill in during a day, I suppose an invalid relies a good deal on memories.'

'Your husband does too does he?'

'No, not much, but he hasn't been in long, and he's still recovering from the operation.'

'He'll come out all right then dear.'

'Yes, I'm sure he will.'

'I seen it all happen before with my mother. But it doesn't make it easier. Sometimes I have the idea that life's the wrong way about, because it's loneliness and pain at the end you see, just when you're the weakest. Doesn't seem fair in a way. And what's last seems to be the flavour for everything; no matter what's gone before.'

'Yes, I suppose it does.'

'If you could just take some of that earlier in your life, not miss it altogether; take your share of that when you're younger, and have some good times at the end. I think about it often. It's strange the ideas you get, isn't it.'

'Of course my mother died at home. A lot did then though didn't they.'

'I think they did.'

'We should be in by now. I make it two now easily.'

'Well almost.'

'Only I haven't got a lot of time you see on Fridays, and I like to spend as much time with him as I can. Do you find that?'

'Yes I do.'

'He was always very busy. He had a very active life really, and he never got used to just passing the time. Men don't, not the way a woman does. You're often busy, but often too you've got to learn to pass the time don't you? Women get the knack of it better I feel. See most of them waiting here are women.'

'Men organise themselves first, and we have to fit in I suppose.'

'That's so. And children. With children you're either run off your feet, or sitting waiting for them. Waiting for them to finish kindergarten or brownies; waiting for them to go to sleep.'

'I do a lot of waiting now he's sick too. He's been in here five months, and before that three and a half months in Blenheim.'

'Yes. The nurse is opening now.'

'I might see you again dear. They're quite strict about it here aren't they. I don't see the need of it: so much as that. But I never did think much of the rules here; it never did seem that much of a place. It's where he is though isn't it, and we can't do anything about that.'

58

In
Foreign Service

A t night the air conditioning was turned off; and there was nowhere left to hide. Hugh opened the wide door into the full bloom of the blue night, and hoped for a breeze. Dainty sweat flies gathered at his neck and wrists. From the gardens sloping away beyond the government hostel he could hear the cries of fruit bats, like badly played violins. Cockroaches appeared as if in answer on the boards.

His eyes were itchy again. A mild fungal disease came in the creases around his eyes because of the sweat. The doctor had told him that Europeans had to put up with it. No-where in all the material he had been given before he came had it been mentioned that the air conditioning was turned off at night in all government buildings. After eighteen months he wasn't reconciled to it, and sat resentful, waiting for a breeze. Yet from long experience he knew that every place is a stranger to its book description, and no lists of facts, however well compiled, approach a feeling of life there.

Hugh heard knocking. He couldn't find the energy to go. 'Come in,' he called. The knocking went on. 'Come in,' he shouted, closing his eyes with the effort of shouting. The project adjutant opened the door, but remained in the corridor. 'Can you see me perhaps,' he said. He spoke formally, but grinned and swayed a bottle of red wine to draw attention to it. The adjutant was carrying his coat as well. The coat was clean, and pale blue, and the adjutant carried it on a hanger. 'I don't like to sweat into good cloth,' he said. The adjutant had a handsome face, yet common in his country.

The skin of his forehead was dark, but his cheeks and nose were lighter, the colour worn thin there.

'I'm trying to muster the energy to do the monthly report,' said Hugh.

'The curse of the seconded Director,' said the adjutant. He put the wire hook of the hanger over the ledge high around the verandah, and his coat hung there, paler against the navy blue of the night. One of the ships in the estuary hooted, and the fruit bats were silenced for a time. The river and the estuary lay like oil in the heat, and at that distance offered not even the effect of coolness.

Hugh liked the adjutant, although he knew that the adjutant had petitioned both governments to withdraw him as agricultural advisor. There was nothing personal in it. The adjutant wanted to control the four thousand equivalent U.S. dollars a month that New Zealand contributed to the project. Not a huge sum, but in this country the discretionary use of funds was the only power that mattered. Adjutant was an odd term for a deputy director of an agricultural project. It was an indication of the respect given to anything military in the adjutant's country. 'What a ridiculous title adjutant is,' said Hugh.

'I have been an adjutant,' said the adjutant. 'When I was a captain in the military.' He seemed to think it a reasonable explanation.

'But for a civilian development project.'

'Ah.' The adjutant said it knowingly, as if Hugh had cleverly changed his position in the discussion.

Hugh took two of the high, old-fasioned glasses that the government hostel provided directors, and the adjutant half-filled them with warm wine. White wine was not common in his country, for it required to be chilled. At military banquets perhaps, thought Hugh, chablis would be drunk by those of sufficient rank. Blossoms were expanding amid the thick leaves of the lisaemm tree. 'Blossoms in the night,' said Hugh. 'Like the African baobab. It's a back to front thing.' The adjutant smiled with pleasure at the wonders of his country.

'As you know it is cooler at night,' he said. 'And we have prolific insect life to ensure pollination.' Full, white flowers they were, that opened with silent abandon in the night. Hugh swallowed wine, and felt sweat run down the side of his chest. 'In New Zealand we have a great deal of grassland,' he began.

'Ah, the expanse of New Zealand grassland,' said the adjutant, from some learning, not knowledge. His English was excellent; lacking only idiom.

'We have a grass-grub there, and for a brief time in the summer it presents in its adult and flying form. At night; that's what made me think of it. On those nights the air is full of them, and their combined droning is like planes in the distance. Nature in the flush of excess can be a startling thing.' When he had left the adjutant's country, thought Hugh, when he had deserted the New Zealand breeding stock and lucerne plots and returned to his own country, it would be impossible to convey there the feeling of the adjutant's land. The fruit bats lamented in the sloping gardens below, the white blossoms of the lisaemm opened against the blue night, and the moths fumbled in the light from his room. 'Once a year,' he said. Once a year dearly beloved, he thought as an echo of his childhood reading. 'The young of a small fish come up the rivers from the sea in runs. Only as long as your finger they are, and almost transparent. We catch them in fine nets on poles, and eat them in fritters.'

'Fritters,' repeated the adjutant.

'Like pancakes. They're too small to clean, and they turn milk white when they're cooked, and their eyes look out of the batter.'

'Intestines and all?' said the adjutant.

'As a boy on the Wairau I saw the Maoris catch them a kerosene tin full at a time.' Hugh wondered why he was telling the adjutant about such national eccentricities.

'I am looking forward to an appointment in New Zealand some day,' said the adjutant. 'The Ministry will send people to select further strains for trials if the programme is a success here. I have never been to a country with pronounced seasons. On the same ground snow in winter, and great heat in summer I am told. Such a variety of climate must be bracing.'

'Very bracing,' said Hugh. The adjutant's slightly dated language created a sense of innocence rather than pomposity. The adjutant's dark eyes were moist, and he was smiling to himself as he imagined the exotic nature of seasons. There was no relief from tropicality in his own country. The lisaemm blossoms had exposed themselves fully, and from the leaves below the first storey verandah a tree frog began its regular clicking. Hugh smiled at the thought that to the adjutant it was New Zealand which was a land of paradox, not his own. 'We have parrots that live in the rocks and snow,' said Hugh, 'and cabbages on trees.'

'I know of the kiwi,' said the adjutant. 'A nocturnal bird with no wings, nostrils at the end of its beak, and hair like a dog.'

Hugh was thinking of the shallow river beds of the east coast; with transient islands of gorse and dry grass, and the pale, yellow clay which blew like pollen when the wind got up. Water was quick, light and cool in those river beds, unlike the oily gleam he could see on the adjutant's estuary.

'Should I discuss business?' said the adjutant. Hugh lifted a hand palm uppermost to show that he didn't mind. The adjutant refilled the glasses with his wine. 'Nothing has come for us again.' he said.

'But I rang the department in Wellington. They had confirmation the shipment reached here.'

'At Customs they say that nothing has come for the project.' The adjutant leant towards Hugh. 'We are expecting equipment from New Zealand I told the controller. Nothing has been received from Europe for the project he told me.' The adjutant laughed. He was able to admit the ineptitude of his countrymen at times.

'We made two gifts to the controller,' said Hugh. 'Didn't we?'

'Indeed.' The adjutant seemed as puzzled as his director. He shook his head to show how inexplicable the situation had become. His handsome face had a light sweat, but he bore the heat without discomfort. The adjutant had been a champion badminton player when he was in the army, but he was a modest man and Hugh had never heard him speak of it. Hugh looked into the breast of the soft, blue night, and told himself it was becoming cooler. 'Two gifts of acceptability,' said the adjutant.

Hugh had grown accustomed to the corruption which accompanied administration in the adjutant's country; but the politics behind it could be more devious. He thought carefully before his next question to the adjutant. 'Who should go and enquire next?' he said. The adjutant smiled, as if to disparage the significance of anything he himself might say.

'The controller likes to deal with the project director. It's a matter of status.'

'I've been. He never admits to me that anything ever arrives.' The adjutant smiled in embarrassment and looked intently into the lisaemm tree.

'The controller,' he said. The lisaemm blossoms in the night were feminine and luminous. 'I feel the controller finds it less difficult to deal with a local person.'

Hugh listened to the clicking of the tree frogs, and thought carefully of the exact words the adjutant had used. It wasn't easy in the heat. The Ministry wanted him to resign, he decided. The Customs were being used as a means of pressure. If he resisted the difficulty of communication would increase until it frustrated any progress on the project. Hugh felt no animosity towards the adjutant. He deserved to be director, and control the remaining four thousand equivalent U.S. dollars a month. The adjutant had a good degree in plant nutrition; and was enthusiastic about the aims of the project. 'Someone who was both director and local would have the advantage in dealing with Customs,' said Hugh.

'Perhaps.' The adjutant shrugged his shoulders. He and the New Zealander were both essentially private men, yet could have regard for qualities of character in each other. Hugh thought that the adjutant was deliberately giving him information now, so that if he chose he could act before the department in New Zealand became aware of any problems in administering the project.

'I have been thinking of recommending that the project be wholly controlled by your own people,' he said.

'We consider it a very worthwhile programme, even on its present scale. Your leadership is most able and practical. I myself would miss such leadership if you went.'

Hugh wished to say that he understood the adjutant's position: that he realized the need for each people to control their own landscape. The heat subdued him though, and he was unable to free himself from the concern for his own comfort. 'At night they turn off the air conditioning,' he said. 'I've never got used to it. Even in Australia I never met this heat and humidity.'

'By eleven it becomes cooler,' said the adjutant, and smiled. A moth struck his hanging jacket, and fell away leaving the imprint of one wing in its own dust. The tree frogs seemed increased in number. Hugh thought that in the morning he would write to New

Zealand, and recommend his withdrawal as director. He would give up the effort to remember the adjutant's country, and return to his home where he belonged. Where no-one knew of the fruit bats or revered the army: where no-one suffered such futile heat, or saw the lisaemm bloom against the night. In time he would cease to believe in it himself perhaps.

The Frozen
Continents

I had never met Beavis before he and I were put on the PEP scheme together. I finished filling in the form promising not to divulge vital and confidential council business which might come my way, and then followed the supervisor to the car. Beavis was already seated. 'This is Beavis,' said the supervisor.

'Typhoon Agnes hit central Philippines on November 5 claiming more than 800 lives,' said Beavis. 'Five hundred on Panay Island alone, 325 kilometres south of Manila; another 45 killed in Leyte and Eastern Sawar provinces.' The supervisor looked away: I said hello to Beavis.

The PEP scheme was an inside one at the museum because it was winter. Where we were taken, however, it seemed colder than out-side. Museums create a chill at the best of times, but in our unused part were ice-floes and penguins. A panorama, the supervisor said. All the penguins were to be handled with care and stored out of harm's way along the wall, but the rest was to be dismantled and carried down to the yard. 'I'll look in tomorrow and see how you're going,' said the supervisor. His nose was dripping in the cold.

'Right,' I said.

'A cold wave at the end of last year claimed at least 290 lives in north and east India. Low temperatures and unseasonal fog and rain caused general disruption to air traffic,' said Beavis with no apparent realisation of irony.

'There's a toilet and tea-room at the west end of the corridor on this floor. Ten-thirty and 3.30,' said the supervisor. He started coughing as he left.

The ocean was what we began on first. As it was plywood it was difficult to recover any sheets to use again. When the water was gone we would be able to move about freely and take greater care with the ice-floes and penguins. I found it an odd sensation at first; standing waist deep in Antarctica as we dismantled it. I pointed out to Beavis the clear symbolism relating to man's despoliation of the last natural continent and so on. Beavis in reply told me that 14 people were killed in a stampede when a fire broke out during a wedding ceremony at Unye in the Turkish province of Ordu.

We had the green sea out by 10.30. Beavis stood shivering by a window we had uncovered and wiped free of dust. He had his arms folded and a hand in each armpit, and he looked wistfully down on to a square of frosted grass, and the neat gravel boundaries. 'It's time for our tea-break,' I told him.

An outline of a hand in felt pen and a list of instructions concerning the Zip were the only decorations on the cream walls of the tea-room: points about not leaving the Zip unattended when filling and so on. I had it read within the first minute, but then words are always the things I notice. There was one failure in agreement of number between subject and verb, but overall the notice served its purpose. I wasn't as confident in assessing the people. They accepted us with exaggerated comradeship as is the response of people in secure, professional employment when confronted with PEP workers, amputees or Vietnamese refugees. I gave my name and introduced Beavis. Beavis had a classy-looking pair of basket-ball boots, and the most hair on the backs of his hands that I've ever seen. 'Army worms invaded the Zambezi valley in the north of Zimbabwe and destroyed maize and sorghum crops over more than 100 square kilometres of farmland,' he said. The museum staff present became more amiable still.

One girl had seductive earlobes and dark, close curls. I had a vision in which I persuaded her to come with me, in which I bit her ear beneath the curls and we made the earth move; or at least shook Antarctica with some vehemence. Instead, all of us apart from Beavis shuffled and spoke of inconsequential things. Beavis had several cups of coffee, then abruptly told us of the 24 bed-ridden people who died in a fire which broke out in an old people's home near the town of Beauvais. Impressively recounted, it subdued us all. I guiltily enjoyed the warmth from the wall heaters and my tea — before going back to the South Pole.

Antarctica had been built in sections and we tried to get as much clean timber and plywood sheets out as possible. As we worked I explained to Beavis the Celtic influence in modern poetry, and he told me of the bush fires in south-east Australia, and the earthquake, six on the Richter scale, which killed at least 20 people in India's Assam state. Beavis had a clear, well-modulated voice, and he was deft with the hammer and saw as well. I thought that he'd probably been one of those students, brilliant and compulsive, whose brain had spiralled free of any strict prescription. We had a rest after managing to strip off the first hessian and plaster ice-floe. The sun gradually turned the corner of the museum, melting the frost from a section of the lawn. It caused a precise demarcation between green and white, like the pattern of a flag. Beavis looked out too; and pondered.

We got on well, Beavis and I, although he wasn't light-hearted at all. As he was releasing one penguin the torso came away in his hands, and left the bum and webbed feet on the ice. Beavis stumbled back on to the discarded timber, exposing the heavy treads of his basketball boots, but he didn't laugh with me; just rubbed his shins and looked carefully down the corridor as if expecting a visitor. 'There's got to be some natural mortality amongst penguins,' I said. 'Put it behind the others and it'll hardly show.'

'More than 100 people drowned when a boat capsized in mid-stream on the Kirtonkhola river near the town of Barisal in Bangladesh,' said Beavis.

I carried armfuls of wood and plaster down to the yard before lunchtime. I experimented with several different routes; partly for variety of experience, partly in the hope of seeing the girl with the dark curls, but she wasn't visible. Somehow I imagined her in the medieval glass and tapestry section rather than in natural history panoramas. I discussed the subject of feminine perfection with Beavis, pointing out the paradox that, in nature as in art, beauty comes not from beauty, but from the combination of the ordinary and the earthly. 'That woman,' I said to Beavis, 'is skin, blood and spittle; that's the wonder of it.' Beavis considered the insight and told me that more than 400 passengers were killed when a crowded train plunged into a ravine near Awash, some 250 kilometres east of Addis Ababa.

Beavis suffered a headache a little before 12 o'clock. I think the cold, and the dust from the penguins, caused it. He sat on a four by four exposed from the display and leant on to the window. His cheek spread out and whitened on the glass. Three times he began to tell me of a tsunami in Hokkaido, but his words slurred into an unintelligible vortex. He burped, and rolled his face on the icy glass. 'It's time for our lunch-break anyway,' I said. He rolled his head back and forth in supplication and whispered ahh, ahh, ahh to comfort himself. The penguins refused to become involved; each retained its viewpoint with fixed intensity. Illness isolates more effectively than absence: I knew Beavis wouldn't miss me for a while so I went to the small staff-room and made two cups of sweet tea, and brought them and the yellow seat-cover back to Antarctica.

The yellow cover draped well around Beavis's shoulders, and he held it together at his chest. He had dribbled on the back of his hand and the black hair glistened there. He sipped his tea, though, and listened while I explained why I had given up formal academic studies, and my plan to use the Values Party to restructure education in New Zealand. I think he was pretty much convinced and I let him sit quietly as I worked. Afterwards he seemed to feel better because he wiped his face with the yellow cover, and fluffed up his hair. He told me about the Bhopal poisonous gas discharge which caused more than 2,500 deaths. 'I remember that one,' I said. There was quite a lot I could say about Bhopal, and I said it as we started on the penguins and ice-floes again. Beavis's preoccupation with recent accidental disasters was a salutary thing in some ways: it minimised our own grievance, made even Antarctica's grip bearable.

The sun made steady progress around the building, and the frost cut back across the lawn with surgical precision. Beavis's affliction passed. I went, in all, 11 different ways down to the yard with remains of the southern continent, but I never saw Aphrodite. I stopped the permutations when a gaunt man with the look of an Egyptologist shouted at me that if I dropped any more rubbish in his wing he'd contact the PEP supervisor.

There's a knack to everything, and Beavis and I were getting the hang of our job. We didn't tear any more penguins after that first one in the morning, yet some of them were soft and weakened, and smelt like teddy-bears stored away for coming generations. I said to Beavis that there'd been too much moisture over the years and that a controlled climate was necessary for the sort of exhibits which had stuffed birds. 'Torrential rain caused flooding and mudslides which killed 11 people and swept away dwellings on the outskirts of Belo Horizonte in the south-east state of Minas Gerais, Brazil.'

Before three o'clock I remembered to smuggle the seat-cover back to the tea-room, and return our cups. I told Beavis that my estimate was that we'd have the whole panorama cleared out inside four days. PEP schemes lasted three months, therefore obviously a good deal of job variety remained — other panoramas to destroy, perhaps. A nocturnal setting for our kiwis, or an outdated display of feral cat species. Beavis made no reply. He was most moved to conversation by literary and philosophical concerns. It was a credit to him really: he had very little small talk did Beavis.

Do not turn off at the wall, it said by the Zip in the tea-room. The Egyptologist was there and he bore a grudge. 'We're going to have three months of this then, are we,' he said. 'A gradual demolition of the institution around us.'

'A Venezuelan freighter was washed ashore in Florida during a storm that caused one death and millions of dollars of damage.'

'For Christ's sake,' said the gaunt man.

The girl with the dark curls didn't come in. The tea-room hardly seemed the same place as that of the morning, but I knew from the writing on the wall that it was. As we went away the Egyptologist had a laugh at our expense. Beavis didn't mind: he trailed his hand on the banisters, and made sure he didn't step on any of the triangles in the lino pattern. Circles were safe, it appeared.

The ice-age was in retreat before us. I had 14 penguins arranged in column of route along the wall, and in the grounds two piles grew — one of rubbish and one of reusable timber. We realised that the sun wasn't going to reach our window, and days start to get colder again in winter after four o'clock. I suggested to Beavis that we leave the penguins in the habitat which suited them, and show our initiative by burning the scraps we'd collected in the yard. We could keep warm with good excuse until knock-off time. I didn't want Beavis to suffer one of his headaches again.

We built a small fire on a garden plot, stood close to it for warmth, and watched the smoke ghost away in the quiet, cold afternoon. Beavis enjoyed the job of putting new pieces on the fire, and I listened as he told of the consequences when the Citarum river overflowed into several villages of Java's Bundung region, and considered myself lucky. The park trees had black, scrawny branches like roots in the air: as if the summer trees had been turned upside down for the season. Deep hidden in the soil were green leaves and scarlet berries.

The museum rose up beyond the yard and the park, but despite all the windows I couldn't see anyone looking out at all. No one to hear us, no one to join us, no one to judge us. The strip of lawn closest to the museum still kept its frost like a snowfall. It would build there day after day. No one to see Beavis and me with our fire. Beavis delicately nudged timber into the fire with his basketball boots, and watched smoke weave through the tree roots. I pointed out to him that we were burning Antarctica to keep ourselves warm, which was an option not available to Scott and Shackleton. 'More than 500 died when a liquid gas depot exploded at San Juan Ixhuatepec, a suburb of Mexico City,' said Beavis.

I felt very hungry by the time the hooters went. Beavis and I had missed lunch because of his headache. If he didn't have something soon I thought he might get another attack because of a low blood-sugar level. My own blood-sugar level was pretty low, it seemed to me. We left the fire to burn itself out, and went three blocks down to the shops. I had enough money for two hot pies, and when I came out of the shop I saw Beavis sitting on the traffic island watching the five o'clock rush. Some people walked; some trotted. Some of the cars had *Turbo* written on their sides and some had only obscure patterns of rust, but they all stormed on past Beavis who was as incongruous there as among the penguins. His lips were moving. I suppose he was reminding the world of earthquakes in Chile, or of an outbreak of cholera in Mali.

I was surprised how satisfied most of the people were, but good on them, good on them. How should they know that the frozen continent was to be found right here in the midst of our city after all.

The Lynx
Hunter

I walk to work. I play all their games: I shall not give them the satisfaction of winning. See me stand respectably dressed by the morning gate and take a japonica sprig to twirl in my fingers, and before my face as I walk. See me smile back to my wife, while anxious, fierce, defeated love pads restlessly between us. Goodbye we say above the rearing cataclysmic opening of the earth: rifts and fumes, scoria of burnt out promises, rose lava blackening, and breaking rose again in fits and starts. A lizard's tongue of aspirations mocked. I shan't be late. Oh I'll be back by five. Failure in the execution of love can be absolved: failure in love's intention is beyond words or relief.

The small birds have gathered by the fence to cheek me more effectively: attack, attack, they sweetly cry. The sky is a child's blue of recollection, and the early sun shimmers as a spider at the corner of its web. That car has passed by twice already: its fat man hopes to see me die. But I'll not fall down here; not weep to darken the smooth asphalt by the Four Square sign. See me twirl my japonica and increase the confidence of stride beneath the asiatic menace of an impassive sky. Good morning Mr Jeffers, and I can reply without a quiver in my voice. There are rice and mushroom specials, tins of cottage garden jam, three of everything for the price of two. Stickers and bunting and flags and games and prizes. I never refer to the malicious faces I see in labels and refracted light; amongst leaves, or massed at partly open doors.

A dromedary is up to its hocks in the pale ocean as it waits beyond the breakwater for the fishing boats to come out to play, and today I shall plan a seminar for forty or forty-five. There will be assembling and registering, name tags and a light lunch free of charge. There will be people allocated to explain both this and that; and role play (do you know all their games?), and assessment and introduction of instructing staff, and simulation exercises. Ah, simulations at the seminar, so rich the ironies of despair. Set down a piece of time for simulation in the span of total simulation. Mirrors catch mirrors catch mirrors, until who cares what images we seek. At last we smile ingratiatingly to effigies in front, while some reality examines the back of our neck.

This is the house I constantly admire; or so it seems to me now. So corporeal and so groomed with stolid care. Each edge of lawn has been precisely found, and like dark residue of sea foam the snail bait rings the tulips. This man must be a master of the game; an expert competitor. He has cornered Pall Mall in whatever monopoly of appearances he plays. The thick orange tiles are allsorts that keep the lid on the house with ease. I feel the spider's warmth on my face from the east; the colours of the sea stir apprehensions. Soft plants bend improbably into the breeze, and defy me to notice the inconsistency. Twirl the japonica, talisman of the customary. See me in this quiet morning as I walk to work. And oh yes, yes, there are watchers. Janissaries ride by to meet their Turkish masters: full of death's defiance and esprit de corps. Birdy, who fell from the monument and died when he and I were twelve, sits by the railway line and smiles at his release from any adult pretence. He wears the brown roman sandals that my mother bought me time after time: the dirt follows the strap line on the skin.

All the sounds of all the world still quiver somewhere in the air, and could break out again. Barabbas, Barabbas, may respond once more; the moas' stupid cry; the laughter of Cleopatra, continental drifted from the Nile; the interminable drumming of Ackroyd's Mill; Savonarola's rhetoric competing with a thousand thousand enquiries of the weather. Good morning, Mr Jeffers. She likes to see inside me, but I have arranged all the features of my face according to Hoyle. I am a match for her, even to recalling Susan and Alastair as names for her children. Her dress lifts to display the pink, unperforated bum which is all that models need, but see I do not even glance away, and could go on for hours with perfectly approved information to match what she believes has happened; is happening; will happen. Masks wear thin; the skull of things shows through. The rack stretches, and the smiles and laughter grow. She says she must let me get on, but I keep a straightforward face. There is the Lynx hunter on her porch; he tries to signal me, but I can see through him. I won't die just here, not talking to this acquaintance past the railway line on my way to work, with the spider's bright heat and the Lynx hunter's appraisal. The passion of my belief is burnt out; seed pods of indefinable species tap against me when I pause. How purposeful are processes of decay. The air is briefly full of thistle-down, each carries an island plea for rescue from the selfsame horror. Breathe shallowly and let them float by.

My daughter pedals past me on her way to school. Affection and recognition animate her face. Ah, the power that convention has over us: the hostages she keeps, like sons of satraps entertained in Rome. The cry of warning is stifled in my throat. I am seized with the fear of some betrayal of that love. I am pledged afresh to the straight and very narrow: to maintain absolute fidelity to every rule I know. A child's trust is the bird of paradise which has no phoenix resurrection. So indeed, Mrs Harrop, indeed. So goodbye, Mrs Harrop, goodbye. I shall see you again, Mrs Harrop, or some simulacrum of that name, and you shall address the guise of Mr Jeffers. Does she wait to see if a bolt protrudes behind my ear, or if I leave strange prints upon the ground. But see me walk on to work commensurate with humdrum expectation, with my japonica to catch the spider's threads. Who knows my shoes are full of blood, and the heart empty of it. My lungs hang like bats within this hollow man. The desolation yawns. Don't look back and don't look down is the high wire's rule, for the Lynx hunter will be watching still.

They are rolling jewels behind me: amethysts and rubies and topaz jostle past me on the slope. Emeralds and diamonds, sapphires and agates, pearls, turquoise, garnets, opals, all compete in splendour. A fragmented rainbow coursed towards the creek by sounds as ordinary as could accompany plain, grey stones. It gathers and spills as vivid seeds into the sunken stream of which the heron is a sentinel. How snugly the tie's knot fits my collar; how snugly the collar fits my neck; how smugly the neck fits between head and shoulders. The water-buffalo wallow amidst the trees and meters of the main street. The mud is a sheen on their massive shoulders, and their movement boils the water. Errors of judgment have been made; pride encouraged me to talk of secret things, to open the nondescript coat we all possess and flash hope as designs. From their cars amid the buffalo the people watch me, half turned away, to see how much longer I can take it. Hello, Hugh, and I am quick with hand and smile to synchronise a greeting. Everything is in its place, yet how Birdy smiles to see me. The world is battened down in case of any storm. I know the way of all the games they play — unless they change the rules. I have learned by rote what it is wise to see. I have become a trustee amongst the inmates of this digest world. Yes, yes, see me. I can walk to work as well as the next man; maybe that next man will be me. There must be no enquiry made of life: stick to compatible descriptions.

For if at night we must lie tightly bound to suffer the other world, at least once more have I made the walk to work without detection. The atlas of our memory retains dark continents: Africas of fear and ecstasy from which we return scathed, old wounds bleeding. In the spider's indifferent warmth, and beneath my asiatic sky, I have walked to work; borne the sacred cripple through a world too opulent to be acknowledged. Good morning, good morning. But what did you expect, what did I expect, what did we expect, of life but this. At least now we know better; which is worse.

See I have reached my work, flipped the last opal from my trouser cuff, opened and closed the door which is perhaps there. Now, Elaine, let us set up this seminar. All right? The cosmic music is unendurably sweet; planets and alpha stars strung on the ice-blue hoops of taut galaxies. The snout of the lava flow smokes by the Farmers' Co-op. Incandescence of roses gleams within its clinker prison. The Lynx hunter is no doubt on watch, yet — psst, psst, help me for I die.

Valley Day

Every second month Brian went with his father on the Big Kick. They drove up the valley and the minister took services at the little church of Hepburn and at the Sutherlands' house. One midday service at Hepburn going up, one in the afternoon at Sutherlands', then the evening drive home. In the autumn the long sun would squint down the valley and the shadows blossom from hedges and trees, and slant from the woodwork of buildings in angles no longer true.

One sermon did the trick on the Big Kick, with only the level of formality altered to suit the circumstances. The minister was relaxed despite the hours of driving, and treated it as a gallant expedition for his son's sake. 'Off on the Big Kick again, eh,' he said. 'The Big Kick.' The scent of the hot motor, taste of finest, stealthy dust, sight of the valley floor paddocks all odd shapes to fit the river flats; and higher in the gullies sloping back, the bush made a stand. Few farmhouses; fewer cars to be met, and dust ahead a clear warning anyway.

Brian had his hand in the airflow and used it to feel the lift on his palm. He assessed the road. Each dip, each trit-trotting bridge, places he would set his ambushes. Hurons or Assyrians swarmed out to test his courage, while his father practiced parts of the sermon or recited Burns and then murmured in wonderment at such genius. Brian made the air take some of the weight of his hand, and he kept his head from the window when a small swamp of rushes and flax was passed in case there were snipers hiding there.

'Will the one-armed man from the war be there?' he said.

'Mr Lascelles. Don't draw attention to it.'

'It happened in the war.'

'His tank was hit, I believe. The arm was amputated only after a long struggle to save it: not until he was back in New Zealand. I visited him in hospital I remember.'

'You can still feel your fingers when you've got no arm,' Brian said. 'They itch and that. If someone stood on where they would be then you'd feel the pain.'

'No,' said his father; but the boy kept thinking it. He saw a cloud a long way off like a loaf of bread, and the top spread more rapidly than the bottom and both were transformed into an octopus.

Hepburn was a district rather than a settlement. The cemetery was the largest piece of civic real estate, and the greatest gathering of population that could be mustered in one place. Mrs Patchett had nearly finished cleaning the church. She was upset because a bird had got in and made a mess, and then died by the pulpit. She said there were holes under the eaves. Even such a small church maintained its fragrance of old coats and old prayers, of repeated varnish and supplication, and insects as tenants with a life-cycle of their own. The air was heavy with patterns of the past: shapes almost visible, sounds brimming audible. An accumulated human presence; not threatening, instead embarrassed to be found still there, and having no place else to go. There were seven pews down one side, and six on the other. Down the aisle stretched two parallel brass carpet crimps, but no carpet in between. One stained window, all the rest were plain, a blood poppy amidst green and blue, dedicated to the Lascelles brothers killed within three days of each other in the great war.

Brian took the bird out on the dust shovel. It left just a stain on the boards behind the pulpit. He threw the bird above the long grass: it broke apart in the air, and the boy closed his eyes lest some part of it fly back into his face. He brought his father's bible, soft and heavy, from the car, and the travelling communion tray with the rows of small glasses set like glass corks in the holes, and the bottle full of the shed blood of Christ.

'Don't wander off then,' said his father. 'Don't get dirty, or wander off. Remember we'll be going with one of the families for lunch.' The boy was watching a walnut tree which overshadowed the back of the church, and ranks of pines behind. He found a place where Indian-like he was hidden, but could look out. He crossed his legs and watched the families begin to arrive. The Hepburn church no longer had a piano, and the man with the piano accordion came early to practice the hymns required. Rock of Ages, and Turn Back O Man. He was shy, very muscular, and prefaced everything he played or said with a conciliatory cough. Fourteen other people came as the piano accordion played. Fourteen adults and six children. Brian watched the children linger in the sunlight before trailing in behind their parents. The one-armed Mr Lascelles came. Even to Brian Mr Lascelles didn't look old. He wasn't all that many years back from the war, and he laughed and turned to other people by the cars as if he were no different. Brian got up and walked about in the pine needles as if he had only one arm. He looked back at the trees he passed, and smiled as Mr Lascelles had done. Without realizing it he walked with a limp, for he found it difficult to match a gait to having one arm.

The accordionist coughed and began to play, the families sang, and the boy stood still at the edge of the trees to see the valley and the bush on the hills. Rock of Ages cleft for me, let me hide myself in thee. He felt a tremor almost of wonder, but not wonder. A sense of significance and presence comes to the young, and is neither questioned by them nor given any name. All the people of that place seemed shut in there singing, and he alone outside in the valley. He could see all together the silvered snail tracks across the concrete path, the road in pale snatches, the insect cases of pine needles drawn immensely strong, the bird's wing in the long grass, the glowing Lascelles poppy in the sunlit window. Rock of Ages cleft for me. Brian tipped his head back to see the light through the pines and the blood ran or the sky moved and the great, sweet pines seemed to be falling, and he sat down dizzy, and with his shoulders hunched for a moment against the impact of the trees. The church was an ark with all on board; it dipped and rolled in the swell of the accordion, and he alone was outside amidst the dry grass and shadows, a sooty fantail, gravestones glimpsed through the falling pines of his own life.

He saw cones. The old cones, puffed and half rotted in the needles were ignored. He wanted those heavy with sap and seed, brown yet tinged with green, and shaped as owls. When dislodged

77

they were well shaped to the hand to be hurled as owl grenades against impossible odds across the road, or sent bouncing amongst the gravestones to wake somebody there. He gathered new stocks by climbing with a stick and striking them from the branches. At first he climbed carefully to keep the gum from his clothes, but it stuck to him anyway, gathered dirt and wouldn't rub away, and lay like birthmarks on his legs and held his fingers.

His father was preaching, for the church was quiet. Brian heaped up a mass of pine needles beneath the trees; working on his knees and bull-dozing the needles with both hands out in front. He built a heap as high as himself, and jumped up and down on it. When he lost interest he left the trees and walked into the graveyard to search for skinks. Quietly he bent the grass from the tombstones, like parting a fleece, and after each movement he waited, poised in case of a lizard. He found none. He imagined that they were destroyed by things that came down from the bush at night. He picked at the resin stains on his hands. Deborah Lascelles, 1874-1932, Called Home. Brian forgot about the skinks. 'Called Home,'' he said to himself. He thought about it as he went down the tree-lined margin of the small cemetery and on to the road. He was disappointed that there were no new cars, but one at least was a V8. He shaded his eyes by pressing his hands to the door glass, in an effort to see what the speedo went up to. He reasoned that anyway as it had twice as many cylinders as their car, it must do twice the speed.

Old now is Earth, and none may count her days. The final hymn. Brian went back into the trees and stood as king on his pine needle heap. He arced his urine in the broken sunlight as an act of territory, and checked the two balls in his pouch with brief curiosity. He jousted against the pines one more time, and brought down a perfect brown-green owl. He ran his hand over the tight ripples of his cone; he hefted it from hand to hand as he went back to the church.

His father stood at the doorway to shake hands and talk with the adults as they left. Those still inside showed no impatience. They talked amongst themselves, or listened with goodwill to what was said by and to the minister. There were few secrets, and no urgency to leave the only service for two months. Mrs Patchett showed Mr Jenkins the holes beneath the eaves, and he stuffed them with paper as an interim measure, and promised to return and do more another day. Things borrowed were transferred from car to car. Wheelan Lascelles stood unabashed, and on his one arm the white sleeve was brilliant against the tan. 'That poem you used,' he said to the minister. 'What poem was that?'

'One of my own in fact.' Brian shared his father's pleasure. They smiled together. The boy edged closer to his father so as to emphasize his affiliation.

'Is that so. I thought it a fine poem; a poem of our own country. I'd like some day to have a copy of it.'

From the sheets folded in his bible the minister took the handwritten poem, and gave it. It was found a matter of interest to those remaining: the minister giving his poem to Wheelan Lascelles. Others wished they had thought to mention it, and strove to recall it.

'We're going to the Jenkins' for lunch,' Brian's father told him when everyone had left the church. The Jenkins lived twelve miles up the valley. The minister preferred having lunch with a family living past the church, for then in the afternoon the trip to Sutherland's was made that much shorter. He let the Jenkins drive on ahead because of the dust, and followed on. 'Mr and Mrs Jenkins eat well,' he said to his son with satisfaction.

On a terrace above the river were the house and sheds of the Jenkins' farm, and a long dirt track like a wagon trail leading in, and a gate to shut behind. 'What have you got on yourself?' said the minister as he checked appearances before entering the house.

'Gum.' Brian rubbed at it dutifully, but knew it wouldn't come off.

'And what's in your pocket?'

'Just a pine cone,' he said. His father flipped a hand as a sign, and Brian took the owl and rolled it away. It lay still warm from his body on the stones and earth of the yard.

'You realize old Mrs Patchett died of course and wasn't there today,' said Mrs Jenkins when they sat down. Brian thought someday he might return and find his pine cone grown far above the Jenkins' home. 'Her mind went well before the end. She accused them of starving her, and used to hide food in her room. The smell was something awful at times.' Mr Jenkins smiled at Brian and skilfully worked the carving knife.

'She wasn't at the services the last time or two,' the minister said. 'I did visit her. As you say her mind seemed clouded, the old lady.' Mr Jenkins carved the hot mutton with strength and delicacy.

'She was a constant trial to them,' Mrs Jenkins said. Mr Jenkins balanced on balls of his feet, and gave his task full concentration. Like a violinist he swept the blade, and the meat folded away.

'I saw Mr Lascelles who's only got one arm,' said Brian.

'Yes, Wheelan Lascelles,' said Mr Jenkins without pausing.

'Old Mrs Patchett was a Lascelles,' said his wife. 'They only left her a short time, but she must have tried to walk back up to where the first house on the property used to be. She went through the bull paddock, and it charged, you see. She wouldn't have known a thing of it though.' With his smile Mr Jenkins held the gravy boat in front of Brian, and when the boy smiled back, Mr Jenkins tipped gravy over his meat and potatoes and the gravy flowed and steamed.

'The second family in the valley were Patchetts,' said Mrs Jenkins, 'and then Lascelles. Strangely enough Wheelan's father lost an arm. There must be long odds against that I'd say. It happened in a pit sawing accident before Wheelan was born.' Brian stopped eating to consider the wonder of it: two generations of one armed Lascelles. On the long sill of the Jenkins' kitchen window were tomatoes to ripen, and a fan of letters behind a broken clock. And he could see a large totara tree alone on the terrace above the river.

'And which was the first European family?' said the minister as he ate.

'McVies. McVies and then Patchetts were the first, and now all the McVies have gone one way or another. McVies were bushmen of course, not farmers, and once the mills stopped they moved on.

'I haven't seen a McVie in the valley for thirty years,' said Mr Jenkins, as if the McVies were a threatened species, fading back before civilization.

'If your father has only one arm then you're more likely to have one arm yourself,' volunteered Brian.

'Play outside for a while,' his father said. 'Until Mr and Mrs Jenkins and I have finished our tea.'

'There's a boar's head at the back of the shed,' said Mr Jenkins. 'We're giving the beggars something of a hurry up recently.'

'There you are then,' said the minister.

The boar's head was a disappointment; lopsided on an outrigger of the shed. It resembled a badly sewn mask of rushes and canvas. False seams had appeared as if warped from inner decay. Only the tusks were adamant in malice; curved, stained yellow and black in the growth rings. Brian reached up and tried to pull out a task, but although the head creaked like a cane basket, the tusk held, and only a scattering of detritus came down. The vision of the bull that murdered old Mrs Patchett was stronger than the defeated head of a pig. The boy sat in the sun and imagined the old lady escaping back to her past, and the great bull coming to greet her.

'What happened to the bull?' he asked his father as the minister topped up the radiator.

'What's that?'

'What happened to the bull that killed Mrs Patchett?'

'I don't know. Why is it you're always fascinated with such things? I don't suppose the bull could be blamed for acting according to its nature.'

As they left amidst the benevolence of Mr Jenkins' smile, and the persistent information from his wife, Brian saw his cone lying in the yard: green and turning brown, and he lined it through the window with his finger for luck, and saw it sprout there and soar and ramify until like the beanstalk it reached the sky. 'A substantial meal,' said the minister.

'There was too much gravy,' said Brian.

'I was born in country like this,' said his father. The bush began to stand openly on the hillsides, and on the farmland closer to the road were stumps which gripped even in death. 'It's awkward country to farm,' said the minister. 'It looks better than it is.' There would be a hut in his pine, and a rope ladder which could be drawn up so that boars and bulls would be powerless below. Tinned food and bottles to collect the rain. Mr and Mrs Jenkins wouldn't realize that he was there, and at times he would come down to the lower world and take what he wanted. 'They tried to make it all dairy country, but it didn't work,' his father said. Brian was willing to be an apparent listener as they went up the valley; mile after mile pursued only by the dust.

Dogs barked them in to Sutherland's. The Oliphants and more Patchetts were already waiting in the main room. There was a social

ease amongst them, arisen from a closeness of lifestyle, proximity
and religion. The Sutherlands had no children left at home; the
last Patchett boy was at boarding school; only the Oliphant twins,
six-year-old girls, were there to represent youth. They sat with their
legs stuck out rebelliously because they weren't allowed to thump
the piano keys. The Sutherlands had a cousin staying who was a
catholic. Brian watched him with interest. There was a mystery and
power in catholicism he thought; a dimension beyond the home-
spun non-conformism that he knew from the inside. Surely there
was some additional and superstitious resource with which to enrich
life. 'Absolutely riddled with cancer,' Brian heard Mr Oliphant tell
the minister.

When the minister was ready the service in the living room began;
there was no more exact timing necessary. Mrs Sutherland played
the piano, and Mr Oliphant enjoyed singing very loudly and badly.
The Oliphant twins refused to stand up with the adults, remaining
in a sulk with their legs stiff before them. Their eyes followed Brian
past the window as he went from the house. He thought the piano
disappointing in comparison with the accordion; more inhibited
and careful, less suited to the movement of leaves and water, to the
accompaniment of birds.

Brian remembered a traction engine from previous visits. Once it
had been used in the mills, but since left in the grass: heavy iron and
brass, and great, ribbed wheels. It was warm from the sun, and
Brian scaled it and sat there. The traction engine had been built
to withstand enormous pressures, and before an age of planned
obsolescence. It was a weathered outcrop; the rust only a film
which didn't weaken, and the brass solid beneath the tarnish. A
land train cast there amidst the barley grass and nodding thistle.
He shifted what levers were not seized, and rocked to suggest the
motion of the engine on the move.

'You get tired of all the services, I suppose?' said the Sutherlands'
cousin. He stood in his carpet slippers, and wore a green woollen
jersey despite the heat. He was almost bald, with just a rim of
coarse, red hair, like the pine needles the boy had heaped up in
the morning. Brian came down to talk. It seemed discourteous
to remain raised up. 'I'm in charge of the afternoon tea. I'm a
catholic, you see.' His eyes were deeply sunk, like the sockets of

a halloween pumpkin. 'I've nothing against your father.' They watched heavy, white geese trooping past the sheds. 'There's cake of course, but you know there's water-cress sandwiches as well. Can you imagine that.' Brian thought it rabbit food, but the cousin was from the city. 'She went and collected it from the creek, just like that. There's wonder still in the world,' he said. 'Did I tell you I'm a catholic?' The cousin began to cry without making any noise, but shedding tears. Brian gave him some privacy by taking a stick and beating a patch of nettles by the hen-run. But the cousin wiped his tears away and followed him. He didn't seem interested in maintaining an adult dignity any more. 'Is that gum on your legs?' he said. The boy told him that he had been playing in the trees at Hepburn.

'There's graves there. One said "Called Home" on it.'

' "Called Home", did it really." The cousin shared Brian's fascination with the phrase. 'Called Home.' He began to laugh: not a social laugh, but a hoarse laugh, spreading downwards and out like a pool. A sound of irony and fear and submission.

Mr Oliphant began shouting 'Earth might be fair, and all men glad and wise'. The cousin listened with his mouth still shaped from the laughter.

'I'd better see to the afternoon tea,' he said. 'There are lesser rendezvous yet. I'll crib another water-cress sandwich if I can hold it down.'

'Peals forth in joy man's old undaunted cry,' they heard Mr Oliphant singing.

'These things are at the end of my life,' the cousin said, 'and the beginning of yours. I wonder if they seem any different for that.' The cousin turned back from the house after a few steps, and came past Brian. 'Jesus,' he said. 'I'm going to be sick again.' He rubbed the flat of his hands on the green wool of his jersey as if in preparation for a considerable task, and he walked towards the sheds. He gave a burp, or sudden sob.

The Sutherlands, Mr Oliphant and the minister came out in search of him when their afternoon tea wasn't ready. Brian could see the Oliphant twins looking through the window. 'Have you seen Mrs Sutherland's cousin?' Brian's father asked him. The boy told him about the crying and the sheds.

'I hate to think — in his state of mind,' said Mr Sutherland. He and the minister began to run. Mr Oliphant saw his contribution best made in a different talent. He filled his lungs. 'Ashley, Ashley,' he cried: so loud that birds flew from the open sheds, and the Oliphant twins pressed their faces to the window. The echoes had settled and Mrs Sutherland had prevented him from further shouting, when Mr Sutherland came back.

'It's all right,' said Mr Sutherland. 'He's been sick again that's all. He's got himself into a state.'

'Who can blame him,' said Mrs Sutherland.

'He was going to make the afternoon tea,' said Brian. 'He started to cry.'

'He's a good deal worse today, but the Rev. Willis is with him.' Mr Sutherland was both sympathetic and matter of fact. 'They're best left alone,' he said. 'Come on back to the house.' Mr Oliphant was disappointed that it wasn't the end; not even a more dramatic approach to the end.

'A sad business,' he said in his lowest voice which carried barely fifty yards. Brian was left to wait for his father. He thought that in that quiet afternoon he could hear Ashley's sobs and his father's voice. He climbed back on to the throne which was the engine, and rested his face and arms on the warm metal.

A column of one-armed Lascelles was moving back up the valley from the war, each with a poem in his hand, and the accordion played Rock of Ages as they marched. Mr Jenkins deftly knifed a wild pig, all the while with a benevolent smile, and in his torrent voice Mr Oliphant Called Home a weeping Ashley: deep eyes and woollen jersey. A host of pine owls, jersey green and brown, spread their wings at last, while old Mrs Patchett escaped again and accused her kin of starvation as she sought an earlier home. Behind and beyond the sway of the accordion's music, and growing louder, was the sound of the grand, poppy-red bull cantering with its head down from the top of the valley towards them all.

Mumsie
And Zip

Mumsie saw the car coming at five, as she had expected. The general noise of homeward traffic was at a distance; but still the desperation was apparent in the pitch of it. Zip always turned off the engine when in the gate, and coasted on the concrete strips until he was parallel with the window. The grass was spiky and blue in the poor light of winter. Mumsie had cacti on the window sill, and the dust lay amid the thorns of Mammillaria wildii.

Zip undid his seat belt, and stepped out. He took the orange, nylon cover from the boot, and began covering the car for the night. He spread the cover evenly before he began to tie it down. Zip always started at the same corner and worked clockwise round the car. He didn't bend to tie the corners as a woman would bend, with backside out, but crouched agile and abrupt, balanced on his toes. Sometimes when Mumsie was close to him when he crouched like that she would hear his knees pop. Mumsie wondered if there would be a day when she would go out and ask Zip not to cover the car because there was something of significance she had to attend: a premiere perhaps, or an apparently trivial summons which would become This Is Your Life, Mumsie.

Mumsie knew Zip wouldn't look up as he came past the window: they always reserved recognition for the kitchen when Zip came home from work. Zip would go to the lavatory, and then to their bedroom to take off his jacket and shoes. Mumsie heard him flush the bowl, and go through for his other shoes.

Zip came to the stove. He stood by Mumsie's shoulder. 'How's things,' he said. The mist of the winter evening was strung through the poles and gables; the thinning hair of a very old woman. Toby McPhedron tried to kick free a flattened hedgehog from the surface of the road.

'Fine,' said Mumsie. 'And you?'

'Busy as usual,' said Zip. 'Just the same, Mumsie. You know how it is.'

'Casserole,' said Mumsie as Zip lifted the lid, 'with the onions in chunks the way you like it. Chunky chunks instead of sliced up thin.'

'Good on you, Mumsie, good on you,' said Zip. 'You know what I like all right.' He rubbed his forehead and circled the sockets of his eyes.

'So the usual day?' said Mumsie.

'You know how it is. Busy of course; always the same.'

'So Mumsie's got a casserole,' said Mumsie.

'You know I like a casserole all right,' said Zip. Mumsie noticed how the pupils of his eyes jittered the way they often did, although his face was flat and still. He stood beside her and looked at the casserole while his pupils jittered.

'You know I couldn't get hardly a thing to dry today. There's no wind and no sun. Hardly a thing dried. I had to take most of it off the line again and put it in the good room with the heater.'

'It's that sort of day,' said Zip. He placed the butter and salt and pepper on the table, and cork mats with the picture of a kitten halting a ball of fluffy wool.

'Mr Beresford died,' said Mumsie.

'Mr Beresford?'

'The place with the new roof; two down from the corner. I heard Mrs Rose talking about it in the shop.'

'Ah,' said Zip.

'So nothing of interest at work today.'

'Uh-huh,' said Zip. He sat down at his place, which was facing the stove and the bench. He laid his hands one each side of his cork mat, as a knife and fork are laid.

'They haven't found the murderer yet,' said Mumsie.

'Murderer?'

'Who murdered those two girls in the boatshed in Auckland. Shaved their heads I think it said. There's a lot of sick things.'

Zip left his hands resting on the table and he looked at the floor by the bench where the pattern on the lino had been worn away. Mumsie's legs plodded this way and that around the kitchen, but always came back to that worn place, on which she shuffled back and forth from stove to table to bench. Zip seemed absorbed: as if that worn patch were a screen and Mumsie's splayed shoes played out some cryptic choreography. But his black eye spots continued to jiggle, and the focus wasn't quite right to hit the worn lino, but aimed deeper, at something behind. Zip sat still, as if conserving energy for a final effort, or as if that final effort had been made to no avail. Mumsie looked at him from time to time. 'Mumsie's done peas shaken in the pot with butter,' she said, 'and baked potatoes in their skins.'

'You're a winner, Mumsie, that's for sure.'

Tears began to form on the windows, and the light outside was fading quickly. 'I like to be in my own house when it gets dark,' said Zip. They could hear persistent traffic noise from the corner, and Toby McPhedron ran a stick along the tin fence next door.

'You don't mind about the heater on in the good room?' said Mumsie. 'There's no drying at all.'

'We can go there ourselves later,' said Zip. 'We'd have to heat one room.'

'Now why would the murderer shave those girls' heads?' said Mumsie.

'Kinky sex, Mumsie. You want to watch out.' Zip watched his casserole with the chunky onions being served, and the potatoes blistered grey-brown, and the peas in butter glistening as emeralds.

Mumsie talked about Mrs Rose's visit to the dentist, about the manner of Mr Beresford's dying third hand, about the boatshed murderer and the good room doorknob which just came off in her hand. The tears made tracks down the windows, and those tracks showed black, or spangled back the kitchen light. Mumsie talked of a party at the Smedley's which they weren't invited to, and how either a niece or a cousin of Debbie Simpson's had a growth in her ear which might be pressing on her brain. Zip said, 'is that right, Mumsie,' and nodded his head to show that he was listening, and in satisfaction as he crunched the casserole onions done in chunks as he liked them: and he kept looking at things deeper than the worn lino by the bench. Mumsie wondered if she should take some pikelets along to Mrs Beresford, or whether she would only be thought nosey because she hadn't really known him. A dog had torn Mrs Jardine's rubbish bag open again, and Mrs Jardine had to clean it up in her good clothes when she came home at lunchtime, Mumsie said.

The winter night, the lizard voice of the traffic at a distance, the condensation on the windows, all intensified the artificial light of the kitchen where Mumsie and Zip ate their casserole, until it was a clear, yellow space separate from the rest of life; independent even from the rest of their own experience, and isolating them there — Mumsie and Zip.

'Mumsie,' said Zip, 'now that was a real casserole, and don't worry about the door knob, because I can get that bastard back on later.'

'I knew you'd like it, being winter and that. And there'll be enough for you tomorrow.'

Zip lit a cigarette as he stood by the bench and waited to help with the dishes. He pulled the smoke in, and his eyelids dropped for a moment as the smoke hit deep in his lungs. In a long sigh he breathed out. The smoke drifted, the colour of the condensation on the window, and Zip had the tea-towel folded over his arm like a waiter and stood before the plastic drip tray as he waited for the dishes. 'I'll put the rest of the casserole in something else,' said Mumsie, 'and then the dish can be soaked. There's always some bubbles out and bakes on the rim.'

'Let it soak then, Mumsie,' said Zip.

'Don't let me miss the start of the news. Maybe they've found the boatshed murderer.' Mumsie liked everyone to be brought to justice. Zip dried the forks carefully, pressing a fold of towel between the prongs. He tapped the ash from his cigarette into Chamaecereus silvestrii on the sill.

'It's just as well we're not in the boatshed belt,' he said.

'But it could be anyone, Zip.'

'Except Mr Beresford, Mumsie. I'd say he must be in the clear.'

'No, I meant it could be any woman. It said on the talkback that these things are increasing all the time.'

Zip spread the tea-towel over the stove top, and shuffled the cork mats into symmetry so that the images of the kittens and the wool were in line. He stood by Mumsie as she wiped the table, and then he sat there and put down a plastic ash tray. Mumsie told him not to pick at the contact because it was already tatty, so Zip rotated his cigarette packet instead; standing it alternately on end and side, over and over again. His fingers were nimble, and the packet only whispered on the table as it turned. 'We'll go through to the good room soon,' said Mumsie, 'seeing the clothes are already in front of the heater there.'

'That's right,' said Zip. He sighed, and the smoke came like dust from deep in his lungs, and drifted in the yellow light. 'Another day another dollar,' he said.

'Just another day, you said.'

'That's right. Another day,' said Zip. He tapped with his finger on the cigarette above the ash tray; a column of ash fell neatly and lay like a caterpillar.

'How many of those have you had today?' asked Mumsie.

'Five or six.'

'Mumsie's going to have to hide them, or you'll be up to a packet a day again.'

'You're a tough lady all right,' said Zip.

'Well Mr Beresford was a heavy smoker, Mrs Rose said, and he wouldn't be told; just kept on. Mrs Rose said in the shop she wouldn't be surprised if that was it.'

'But you don't know it was smoking Beresford died of.'

'It can't have helped,' Mumsie said. Zip continued to turn the packet with his free hand, head over heels it went again and again. Mumsie said that she'd heard that a lot of drugs had been found in the fire station, but it was all being hushed up. Mumsie enjoyed her delusion of occasionally sharing privileged information. 'It'll all be swept under the carpet because they know each other, all those people, you see if they don't.'

'They'd bloody well come down on you or me though, Mumsie, that's for sure,' said Zip.

Mumsie was talking about the food specials at Four Square when the phone rang. She was comparing for Zip the large coffee with the giant and the standard. Standard meant small, but nothing in supermarkets is labelled small. Zip remained still, apart from turning the cigarette packet. He paid no attention to the phone: he had no hope of it. He was unlucky enough to know his own life. But Mumsie was quite excited. She wondered who that could be she said, and she tidied her hair as she went into the passage. Zip didn't alter just because Mumsie had gone. He stayed quietly at the table as if relaxed, turning the cigarette packet. He did work his mouth; pulling his lips back first on one side then the other, as a horse does on the bit. Zip looked at the table, and the worn lino by the bench, and Mumsie's cactus plants which could survive her benign forgetfulness, and at the windows decked with tears; and his eyes jiggled.

Mumsie was happy when she bustled back in. She felt things were going on. There were decisions to be made and she was involved, and someone had taken the trouble to phone her. 'It's Irene and Malcolm'' she said. Zip let out a dusty breath. The tears of condensation left black trails on the windows, and a small rainbow bubble winked as Mumsie shifted the detergent flask. 'They're going to stay for a few days next week,' said Mumsie. 'Malcolm's got some management course again.'

'No,' said Zip.

'Why's that?'

'I don't want them here. I don't want them here next week, or next year, or ever. I don't want other people in my house, Mumsie. Got it? I don't want Malcolm and his moustache telling me how well he's doing, and your sister making you look like Ma Kettle all the time.' Zip didn't raise his voice, but there was in it a tone of finality.

'But they're family,' said Mumsie. She turned the water on and off in the sink for no reason.

'They're not coming. You're going to tell them that they can't come, or I'm going to. You'll do it nicer than me.'

'How often do we have people?' said Mumsie. 'We never see anyone.'

'I don't want to see anyone, and I don't want anyone to see me. People are never worth the effort, Mumsie, but you never seem to learn that.'

'I get sick of no-one coming. I get sick of always being by ourselves,' said Mumsie.

Zip spread the corners of his mouth in one grimace of exasperation, and then his face was flat again. 'You're stupid,' he said. 'What are you?'

'Maybe I am,' said Mumsie, 'but I've got a life too. I'm not too stupid to have my own sister to stay am I.'

'You're a stupid, old bitch, Mumsie, and I'm as bad. In a way I'm worse because I'm just bright enough to see how stupid we both are, and how we're buggered up here like two rats in a dung hill. We've got to keep on living our same life over and over again.'

'Oh, don't start talking like that, and getting all funny.' The windows were black eyes shining with tears, and the custard light of the room grew brighter in contrast with deep winter outside. The table legs cast stalks of shadow across the floor, and high on the cupboard edges the fly dirt clustered like pepper spots. 'Anyway, I've told them they can come, and so they can,' said Mumsie. She pretended that by being emphatic she had made an end of it, but her face was flushed and her head nodded without her being aware of it.

Zip eased from the seat, and took a grip of Mumsie's soft neck. He braced his body against hers and he pushed her head back twice on to the wall. Mumsie's jowels spread upwards because of the pressure of Zip's hand, and trembled with the impact of the wall. Their faces were close, but their eyes didn't meet. The sound of Mumsie's head striking the wall echoed in the kitchen; the mounting for the can opener dug in behind her ear. Mumsie began to weep quietly, without any retaliation. 'Now I tell you again they're not coming,' said Zip. He sat back at the table, and began to turn the cigarette packet top over bottom. Mumsie put her hand to the back of her head for comfort, and her fingers came back with a little blood.

'I swept out the storeroom today, Mumsie,' Zip said. 'I swept out the bloody storeroom when I went to that place twenty years ago, and today I swept it out again. I was doing it when the buyers came and they all went past me and into Ibbetson's office. Ibbetson didn't say anything to me, and neither did any of the buyers. I'm the monkey on a stick.'

'I thought you liked my sister,' said Mumsie. She dabbed at the blood with a paper towel, but Zip didn't seem to notice.

'I'd like to screw her, Mumsie, you know that, but she wouldn't let me, and there's nothing else I want to have to do with her apart from screwing her. She's up herself, your sister.'

'You're just saying it.'

'I'm just saying it and it's the truth. We make a good pair, you and me, Mumsie. We don't take the world by storm. Two stupid people, and if we stopped breathing right now it wouldn't mean a thing.'

'It would to me,' said Mumsie.

'We're dead, Mumsie,' said Zip.

'Don't say that.' Mumsie watched Zip, but he didn't reply. He seemed very relaxed and he looked back at the watching windows, and his eyes jittered. Mumsie didn't like silences: talk was reassuring evidence of life moving on for Mumsie.

'You're that proud,' said Mumsie. 'You're so proud, and that's the matter with you. You'll choke on your pride in the end.'

'You might be right there, Mumsie,' said Zip. 'Most of us could gag on our own pride.'

'You hurt my head then you know. It's bleeding.'

'You're all right. Don't start whining. I'll have to hit Ibbetson's head one day, Mumsie, and then there'll be hell to pay.'

'Oh, don't talk about things like that.'

'It's going to happen. Some day it's bound to happen, and there'll be merry hell to pay.'

'Why can't you just be happy, Zip?'

'I'm not quite stupid enough, more's the pity. I can watch myself; and I don't bloody want to.'

'Let's go into the good room,' said Mumsie. 'We'll push the clothes out of the way and sit in there in the warm.'

'Sure, but first Mumsie we'll have a cuddle in the bedroom. I quite feel like it, so you get your pants off in there and we'll have a cuddle.'

'It's cold in there,' said Mumsie.

'You get your pants off, Mumsie,' said Zip. 'You know what your murderer did to the boatshed girls — shaved their hair all off, so you want to watch out.'

'It's awful. I meant to watch it on the news to see if they've found him.'

'You can't trust anyone but your family, Mumsie. You've got to realize that.'

'I suppose so.'

Mumsie kept on talking so that Zip would forget to tell her again to go into the bedroom and take her pants off. She told him that after Mr Beresford died the blood came to the surface of his body, so Mrs Rose said, and his face turned black and his stomach too. 'Maybe it was the tar-brush coming out,' said Zip. She told him about Mrs Jardine claiming the family care allowance even though their combined income was over the limit. She told him again that the doorknob had come off in her hand, and about the niece or cousin of Debbie Simpson's who had a growth in her ear and they might have to operate because it was pressing on her brain and making her smell things that weren't really there. 'What a world,' said Zip. He ran his thumb and forefinger up and down the bridge of his nose, and his eyes jittered and their focus point was a little beyond anything in the kitchen. He lit another cigarette, and Mumsie didn't say anything about that, but went on talking about who did Mrs Jardine think she was just because they both worked and she could afford plenty of clothes.

The light was banana yellow, and the windows like glasses of stout, beaded with condensation. Mumsie had a magnetic ladybird on the door of the fridge, and the one remaining leg oscillated as the motor came on. Zip had no question on his face, and his hands lay unused on the table before him. 'Mumsie's going to tell you now that I made some caramel kisses today as a treat,' said Mumsie.

'You're a Queen,' said Zip. 'You're a beaut.'

'And we'll have another cup of tea, and take it through to the good room with the caramel kisses.' Mumsie brought the tin out and opened the lid to display the two layers of kisses. 'They've come out nice and moist,' she said.

'They look fine, Mumsie,' said Zip. 'You know I like a lot of filling in them.'

'I made them after I'd been to the shop,' said Mumsie. 'It'll be warmer in the good room, and the clothes should be dry.'

When the tea was made, Mumsie put it on a tray. She was pleased to be going at last to the good room. She paused at the door. The blood was smudged dry behing her ear. 'Bring in the caramel kisses for me,' she said.

'Sure thing, Mumsie,' said Zip. He heard Mumsie complaining about there being no knob on the good room door.

'This bloody door, Zip,' said Mumsie. Zip cast his head back quickly and made a laughing face, but without any noise.

'All right, Mumsie,' he said. 'I'll come and do it now,' but he stayed sitting there; his hands on the table, his face still once more, and only his eyes jit jittering as bugs do sometimes in warm, evening air.

Joining
The Ishmaelites

True literary achievement depends upon extremes in life; the gathering of emotional and social copy. I know this from my reading, and television interviews with pub troubadours. Middle class existence is the kiss of death for a writer. Life has to be experienced in a way which bares the soul, guarantees a natural expression of emotion and an individual response. Then in your up-stairs lodgings that experience can be dragged through the type-writer, still reeking of authenticity, of stoic resilience, of hat brims turned down against the drizzle of another lonely night. Jack London did it; and Maupassant, Orwell, Babel, Laurie Lee, Melville and Sargeson.

I also am planning to do it. I've been planning to do it for some time. I've had a small tattoo of an eagle with a snake in its claws, done on my shoulder, and I've considered the sort of jobs that provides copy for a writer. Stevedore is fine; being a municipal rat-catcher in Seville is better. Male stripper, geek, trucker's mate, lob-lolly man, night duty morgue attendant, SAS instructor, Punch and Judy man, reptile house curator, nassella tussock grubber, T.V. gaffer, merchant seaman, barman, drover, torch singer, possum trapper, ringer, kakapo ranger, extra on the remake of The African Queen: these are jobs that will come up with the goods for anyone with talent.

But only for a year or so. It is another kiss of death to stay longer — stultifying to the gathering of reeking copy, and suggesting an ingratiating concern for things apart from writing. Being declared redundant, or better still being fired, is the right way to leave: defying morgue officialdom with an astounding display of curt eloquence, while the light from one hung bulb throws shadows on both the living and the dead. Standing on principle, or up for a mate with seven Polynesian sons. Proving you can do your share with the best, but then moving on: turning up your collar against life, and pausing only on the bridge above the city to hear the freight train's whistle dying through the fog. Alone again, except for your memories and your copy: on the road again.

Accounting, plastic extrusion, advertising, law, real estate, dentistry, haberdashery, government service at greater than subsistence level, are the ways in which genius and literary commitment are bled away. Such occupations cast a glaze of complacency and triviality on life: they involve keeping the rules, ratting on your mates, mortgages, and remaining the father of your children. You name me one writer of significance who has been branch manager of BNZ, or a chartered accountant, or mayor. No, there's only the one way; the Hemingway, the way of Gogol and Kesey, of Powys and Frame, of Faulkner, Saroyan and Sherwood Anderson. The gaunt, solitary and self-sufficient way on the cutting edge of society. Ishmael's vision, purged by angst and victimisation; pared down by hardship.

In preparation for the true literary life, I have begun to expose myself. On winter evenings I walk to the gravel pits by the tannery. I can scent the tannery, stand amongst the scattered ice-plant and scabweed, and experience feelings of the waste of human potential, alienation, and the age old tyranny of man's inhumanity to man. I may recite to myself from Dylan Thomas's Hunchback in the Park, or some lines from Schopenhauer. Things rust nicely in the gravel pits because of the salt air, and are etched to poignant commentaries of transcience and futility.

Or I visit the Salvation Army emergency shelter: not to help, but to stand in solidarity with those resolute individualists in streaked gaberdine coats done up with twine. I know what it is to be demeaned; to stare up with them at the underbelly of leviathan society which threatens to crush us all. Oh, I have innumerable authentic backdrops stored up within my mind.

Nicaraguan mercenary, fitch breeder, brakeman, mummer, gumdigger, light-house keeper, rigger, pimp, mutton birder, scrub cutter, land marcher, busker, barker, glass blower, Linters' knave, male nurse at Oakley: these are more of the jobs I need to keep in mind. The eye of literature's needle is even more select than religion's: no tax collectors, no air hostesses, no continuity announcers or hair stylists, no Secretary for Tourism, no barristers, brokers, or brigadiers, no professors once death has removed the need for deference. All the names that last have taken Ishmael's way — Steinbeck and Synge, Lawrence and Pritchett, Conrad, Coppard and Crane. The Brontes faced down the daemons of the heath: O'Connor and O'Faolain traced the desolate moor.

I am ready for the grim and reticent comradeship of men who have descended to the bowels of society. I'm ready for the mournful horns of ships passing in the mist, and the lone, astringent cry of the morepork or whip-poor-will on dipping, country roads. I'm ready for the purgatories of furnaces and canneries where sweat and toil bring apocalyptic revelation. I'm ready to reject the blandishments of materialism — when I have the opportunity; and to make greater sacrifices, let soft fingers trail reluctantly away from my tattoo. I'm ready to be the stranger in the valley, with the slight, ironic smile.

In every town or city there are to be found two uneven groups; not young and old, not men and women, not Catholic and Protestant. I mean the real distinction — those on the inside, and those on the outside looking in. Those citizens who place slug-bait in their gardens, have their numbers in the phone book; and those few who leave messages with Mac at the Railway Hotel, and know the dry place in the brick works if the weather turns nasty. The majority may see occasionally from the mundane and complacent comfort of their hedged community, a hard, spare man pause by the family gates in the evening to listen to the children's voices, then shrug and carry on with the last leaves of fall a shadowed eddy about his feet. It's all copy; all reeking copy to those Isherwood eyes.

The time is near when I will feel that I'm prepared to begin that journey. I'll take my last cards into Miss Tombs, who heads circulation, and she will like to ask me more, but be deterred by something austere in my expression. And I'll take my coat and just one grab-all, and walk to the bus station to begin my search for character and copy. There'll be no-one to see me go: no embrace or soft farewell to begin the writer's lonely business. Yet even Ishmael begot a race, and the Jacks London and Kerouac, Gissing and Turgenev, all went the selfsame way. One small child by the kiosk may look up and wonderingly catch my eye, as the urban tumble-weeds of crumpled paper flicker by. A window seat well back within that unremarkable bus with its few passengers. And the bus will pull out, and through the cold rain speckled on the glass I will look my last upon the town that I was born in. For I will have begun my writers' life at last: inexorable bounty hunter of reeking copy — and fame.

Melodrama
At Closing Time

Scene I

THE PREMIER is speaking on the phone. He stands in the ante-
room before joining the formal banquet; and his mistress is close
beside him with her hand in his shirt. The golden tasselling on his
epaulettes trembles slightly. The Premier says, 'In five minutes I
have to go in there and talk to all those jerks. I have to look past
their tossed salad and poulet, and tell them this great country is
getting great again. And Al, I need to sell it with ideas, not goddam
computer read-outs. Convictions, Al, know what I mean?' The
Premier cups his hand over the mouthpiece: he smiles at his mistress.
He is an impressive man, and all his teeth are evenly capped and
white. His smile is slow, almost rural in impact, and redolent of
uprightness, sincerity and determination to keep the country great
again even at personal sacrifice. 'Yes honey,' he says to his mistress,
'you've got me there. Keep paddling baby,' and his mistress giggles.
Her blond hair drapes the insignia of his chest, and the tasselling
shivers on his shoulders.

The Premier takes his hand from the mouthpiece. 'I know you'll
come through for me, Al. I know that you'll have a speech for me
next week that'll bounce the people off their bums; that'll give us
emotional momentum again. The biggie is to be that nation-wide
on Tuesday, Al. You come up with the goods, and I'll deliver them.
I'll be waiting. These jerks tonight I can roll over anytime I like.
Jesus, I'm a politician aren't I!' The Premier laughs into the phone,

which occupies his voice, takes a grip of his mistress's blond hair, which satisfies his libido, and looks from the ante-room into the crouching night.

Electric light in the hallways is redoubled by the rows of faceted chandeliers, and the light cascades from the windows and balconies of the Castle and rides on the fur of the night. 'Attaboy, Al,' says the Premier, and he is thinking who he will get to replace Al when the time comes. 'No-one writes conviction the way you do. People are all suckers for a good line.' The Premier replaces the phone. 'That College boy's all spectacles and goddam teeth,' he says. 'Got no hair on his body at all.' His mistress giggles and works harder. 'I hate the smart arsed jerk,' says the Premier, and he starts to smile again.

Scene II

AL has a tennis shade over his forehead, and he is wearing a russet, slim-line jersey. Most of the wall behind him is covered with diplomas and presentations. He is giving instructions to his brother. 'Buy 20,000 Media Specs, and dump Evangelical Associates. And Wallace, get that money moved off shore for christsake; get it moved off shore fast. You know how quick these exchange rates can alter.'

Al is used to working twelve hours a day. He goes through to his personal rooms next to the offices, and he keeps talking to Wallace as he changes into his track suit. He jogs down corridor level 17, and down the west stairs to corridor level 16, and along that as far as the east stairs back to level 17. Each circuit takes two and a half minutes, and as he runs he talks to Wallace back in the office by way of his chest microphone.

'You know Wallace,' he says, 'I reckon we've about four months before that anthropoid slips us the knife, and appoints his favourite talk back host.'

'Can we make it through the Jacobsen enquiry?' says Wallace from his desk. He is using the computer to devise an inventory of his World War Two artillery shellcase collection. Al's voice comes back without any sign of effort; the microphone catches just the slight slap of itself on Al's chest as he jogs along corridor level 16. 'Affirmative, Wallace,' he says. 'You see, the play-offs are at the same time by no coincidence, and I've asked outer zone governors to move their executions to the same week. You know what the ratings of those two things are! Who the hell's going to bother watching the Jacobson enquiry.'

'Physicals or mind blanks?' says Wallace. Al runs past the office doors: he and Wallace can see each other for a moment.

'Physical executions,' says Al into his chest as he turns towards the stairs. 'You know that ideologically I'm opposed to it, but as they're going on, then I'm damn sure that's the right time.'

'Right,' says Wallace.

After two more circuits Al speaks to his brother again. 'More convictions the man wants, to make spells with. More ideas, more snappy stuff to keep this country great again. I'd say we've got four months, Wallace. Keep moving the money off shore, and don't be tender about collection. We haven't the time. Let the little people feel the need.'

'Whatever you say.'

'I haven't worked for three post-graduate degrees to be left dusting off my pants when a fall guy's needed.' Al comes into the office, and takes a towel from his brother to put round his neck and tuck into his sweat shirt. He runs a quick surveillance check on the computer to make certain there are no bugs or long range snoops. 'Get all the slush fund and credit monopoly material ready to drop to the media if need be. Leave a trace back to the Alternative Feminist Government, or perhaps the Democratic Fundamentalists. Nothing too obvious.' Al goes through to his shower, and strips off. He begins his neck exercises as the warm, blue grade water flows over him. 'We need some grass roots conviction for next Tuesday's speech, Wallace: some soul, something with a tint of honesty. We write speeches remember. That's our department.'

'Soul, conviction, honesty? Where do such things reside,' says Wallace. He has started with the computers on the slush fund data, but he finds time to smile.

'There is still the exception: the magnificently naive man, who takes a myth as his vision, and makes it come true. Yea, jot that down, Wallace, we might use it.'

'I'm expecting to hear from our source in State Corrections,' says Wallace. 'We might yet get a little soul given up for a speech.'

Scene III

THE FREE RANGING DISCUSSION GROUP is meeting. Seven people gather in Esmeralda's flat in a pink water, semi-radiation district. Esmeralda has a small table of real wood. It shines beneath the one bulb, and the knot in its grain which gathers the cooking oil she uses as polish, is dark as the pupil of an eye. Pignatti comes stamping in on his artificial foot, and he trails his hand on the table's surface before sitting on the floor mats with the others. 'Real wood,' he says.

'Our permit has been extended,' says Esmeralda. She can't keep the good news to herself any longer. 'I had to spend hours with the cultural official,' she says, 'but he agreed finally that ours was a long standing artistic group with no political history.'

'I'm told he's fairly long standing himself,' says Pignatti, but Esmeralda pretends not to hear. 'I'm told that all government services have been withdrawn from three more zones as well,' he says.

'Out of order,' says Esmeralda. 'No politics. Constitution quite clear on that.'

'Is it bread or rice next week?' says one of the others to ease the tension.

'Bread week and transfusion week,' says Esmeralda.

'And de facto support week.'

'No, no. Don't you ever listen to the bulletins,' says Esmeralda. 'Hinder assassins week: de facto support's the one after, which is also a rice, fight AIDS, eradicate pets and folklore recollection week.'

There is a noise far away, like a bagpipes festival distorted in the wind. The mobs are chasing uncertified women in the old dock area again. No-one makes any reference to it. 'Do you realize,' says Peter, 'that there are probably less than 300 tundra bears still in existence.' Esmeralda is filled with horror at the plight of the tundra bears. Another tender-hearted member of the group begins to weep. Pignatti screws his false foot back and forth. 'We must raise funds for the Government Tundra Bear Appeal,' says Peter. The security strobes of the passing patrols play briefly across the windows.

'Let's get to our Shakespeare then,' says Pignatti.

'We should first finalise our logo,' says Esmeralda.

'We're always talking about the logo. God almighty.' Pignatti knows his objection won't be supported, and so he speaks wearily.

'Yes, but we haven't decided on the colours, and if it's to be bas-relief, and whether a matt or gloss finish,' says Esmeralda.

'I move, madam chair, that we remain in plenary session to debate the logo.' All except Pignatti agree with Peter, and they settle to so spend their time.

Scene IV

THE CORRECTIVE COUNSELLOR is at work on the opposite hill to that lit up by the Premier's palace. The Counsellor's hill is tapered like a throat, with the lights of the city strung at its base. Nevertheless the research centre on the summit is a place of serious activity. One of the Counsellor's responsibilities is the testing of Government tenant Lupassin; and the Counsellor takes that duty seriously.

He adjusts the flash under Lupassin's ear lobe, and she strains on the brace so that tendons and veins alter the configuration of her face. 'When does it all end, my dear,' says the Counsellor quietly. It is some time before Lupassin regains sufficient control to lift her eyes to him.

'There are never any real beginnings, or endings, any departures or arrivals,' she says. 'There are just emotions and associations which like the profile of a wave, pass and leave the ocean as it was.'

The Counsellor seems preoccupied with his machines. Through the narrow windows, open to heat and pain, the curfew dogs are heard whining eagerly as they trot down the hill towards the parks. The Counsellor raises his eyebrows, and wipes sweat from above his eyes with the muscle at the base of his thumb. He rests by one of the windows for a time, and observes the city. Heaped pearls and diamonds of light upon the night, and the main streets outlined with rubies. It is strangely tender: the rush, stink and relentless competition are at such a distance transmuted to a jewelled pulsing.

'Shall we talk of your idea children,' the Counsellor says. 'Two still live.' He holds a terminal on the wet place beneath Lupassin's nose, and the shock flays back her hair. He balances the effect with a yellow drug visually ingested. 'I said two still live. Can you remember them.' The tenant tries to work her lips: they flutter and warp of their own volition.

'Yes,' she says finally.

'Yet you forget the other things it would be convenient to know.'

'Pain purges everything but love,' says Lupassin in a lilting voice of the drug. 'Only daughters, lovers, creations and sacrifices are remembered at the last.'

'What else do you love?' enquires the Counsellor. The guest of the state thinks for a time, making the most of the respite. One eye is very bloodshot. 'What else is dear to you?'

'Hope,' says Lupassin. 'I love hope for it is the most enduring form of resolve.'

'Who do you remember especially as having hope?' says the Corrective Counsellor. Lupassin's face becomes wry. Even though she is dying and has the drug, she recognizes a lack of subtlety unusual in the Counsellor, and he acknowledges it by shifting the subject.

'All those notions you people had,' he remarks. 'Things are different now.'

'Most men will do anything with a clear conscience provided they find themselves united in their views. When all consensus is suspect, only individual and absolute morality has any value.'

'Go on; go on,' says the Counsellor. He applies deft pressure with the sodium skewer, but Lupassin takes a breath that seems to vanish in for ever; then a noisy catch. Her hands bob, and are still. Her breath eases out. The Counsellor observes the awareness of self in her eyes retreat. He recognizes a moment of interrogation more profound than even his skills approach. 'Ah, well,' he says softly. He lights a cheroot, watches the city below for a time, then rings the private number. 'I have some last words. Just a short, routine tape, but you may be interested: might come across something.'

'Send it over,' says Wallace.

Scene V

THE PREMIER occupies the rostrum in the great conference hall. He is ringed with technical equipment and personnel of the media. The long rows of delegates, plenipotentiaries and ratified observers are at some remove. The Premier's plea to those still being issued with credits to support the National Tundra Bear Appeal has been masterly. As the applause abates, he lets his eyes drop to his speech notes as an indication of modesty, and his face has an expression of forebearance and responsibility to suggest the burden of keeping his great country great again.

Every second window is open, but strobe protected against snipers. From the tropical night moths and varangian beetles are attracted by the magnificence of the lighting, and then overcome by it. The Premier's broad tunic glints with the medals won by acts of courage before his rise to power. He begins again, his voice resonant. 'Whatever enemies and obstacles arise before us, we will not succumb. We will not stand by and see our traditional way of life destroyed. I am pledged to you in honour to keep this country great again; with God's help and with yours I will endure until that pledge is redeemed.'

The Premier dips his noble head slightly to the cameras, but does not look away. The delegates and plenipotentiaries watch respectfully from their rows. Microphones and cameras swivel, gawk and stretch on their booms about the rostrum. In a brief flurry in the grounds below the castle, an intruder is garroted by the patrols. It passes unnoticed by the guests in the hall. 'Isn't it true that whatever temporary measures and policies it has been necessary to invoke, our ideals have remained unaltered; our political vision unchanged. There are never any real beginnings, or endings, any departures or arrivals. The exigencies of the day like the profile of a wave, pass and leave the essential nation as it was.' The dark summit of the opposite hill where the Counsellor works, is barely visible against the night sky.

'Let us hold resolutely to our abiding beliefs,' says the Premier. 'Many people will do anything with a clear conscience provided they find themselves united in their view, but let us maintain an absolute morality whatsoever the cost; for pain purges everything but love. And let us link hope with love, for hope is humanity's most enduring form of resolve.' An outburst of applause. A tear of genuine organic origin glitters on the Premier's cheek in the midst of his oratory. Three varangian beetles swing in an elliptical orbit about the chandelier above him. 'I cherish a dream,' says the Premier. 'A dream of this great country great again; a dream of families and flowers; of God's plenty and Man's stewardship of it. A dream which transmits the past and guarantees the future, if only we can be steadfast in this present time.'

The vast hall is quiet: the media technicians crouch submissively amidst their masters: the words are carried out powerfully as the Premier feeds the nation.

Chevalier

So he comes, armoured crusader diminished only by perspective, drifting through vibrations of mirage. Convections well away; the ripple patterns of decaying vision which are harbingers, and presumed reality twists and floats. Change the climate of analogy and the aurora is his prefigurement; flickering veils across the desolate periphery of sight. Comes the Chevalier.

Foreboding is a taste of things expected. Rising in the throat it brings more frequent swallows. The blood moves back to protect the bulk, the heart, and the face whitens. The strange beauty of a dappled, falling world is perceived only from experience as pain. So await the Chevalier.

Bargains are of no avail with a mercenary of such scruples. Draw the drapes as for a tryst and wait, hidden not from him but from the light. Dungeons are the sites of torture, yet it is the existence of the latter which creates the first. Burp out a welcome upon the rack for the impavid knight. Prepare a bowl for offerings. Obeisance in the presence of the Chevalier.

Perpetual warrior, he is here without invitation; at last. The tip of his lance an unassailable greeting placed in the left eye socket and angled up into the brain. Hear the creak of harness as his practiced horse leans to its task. Who is Saracen now to the Chevalier?

All things held dear, all admiration, qualities, lovers and skills are cast away. Torment is a unique priority, and pain the absolute form of isolation. Keening may be an accompaniment, not consciously, but disembodied it seems to suit the time whether petition or protest. Release is sought on any terms from the Chevalier.

No compassion is ever known from Sir Migraine, but detected through familiarity at least a sense of resignation: a professional detachment from the nature of his work. How well he couches a lance. Only metaphorically the point of it all escapes me. To humble us perhaps, or force tribute to a liegelord we fail unwittingly to recognise. Chocolate and red wine are absurd as justification for such punishment. Or does he come with genealogical warrant, the blame laid far back, the penalty exacted now? The character of us all is fragile; elaborated from organic chemistry instead of principle, as illness reveals. So courage may be just an active gland, and deceit a hormone deficiency.

Some death, some part of dying in life, may be a useful admonition. Those whom the Chevalier visits are made sober by it. Yet the nub is not the reason for his coming, but the significance of his arrival. And the stomach cramps again, again: the bile tinged with blood at last will show, the lance point scratches at the tender bone, eyelids flutter in false ecstasy. The Chevalier is about his business. Ah, he is here, my fell Chevalier.

The Republic
In Decline

Cold and broken weather early in September. The Rev. Willis had a heater on in his study. He was choosing texts and hymns for Sunday. The shrubs outside the window tossed in the southerly gusts. The Rev. Willis left his heater and study reluctantly when the phone rang. He stood in the chill hall of the parsonage and looked at the uneven coathooks he knew so well below the stairs. 'How long ago was this, Mrs Trott?' he said.

'It would be Tuesday in the afternoon. It was Mrs Miller next door that said to ring you. We're not regular attenders or anything see, though I have been meaning to.'

'You have no wish to bring the police in, Mrs Trott?'

'She won't hear of it. She's in a proper state I'd say. He's been belting into her again you see.' The Rev. Willis stood alone in the long hall and regarded the coathooks from habit. 'I feel awful ringing you at all actually,' Mrs Trott said, 'but I don't know what else to do.'

'I'll come round right away.' He went back to his study. He turned off the heater, and folded the sheet of texts and hymns under his desk calendar. He put on his gaberdine topcoat, soft with age, and went out to the garage.

The front tyres were worn. The Rev. Willis inspected them, and an oil stain on the garage floor. He tried to remember if the oil stain was smaller on the last occasion he had noticed it. He took a tomato stake from the bench and scraped at the stain to see how fresh and thick it was.

At Chaeroneia Sulla was outnumbered three to one, and Archelaus a worthy general to contend with. Yet Sulla trusted to his legions; and to his luck. Epaphroditus he called himself in Greece, Felix in Rome. A master of the counter-attack was Sulla, and never lost his nerve. The Boeotian hills resounded to his success: his men would follow anywhere he led. They loved a hard man. He was much like themselves, and a lot of other things besides.

The Rev. Willis remembered he was in a hurry, and placed the stake on the bench again. He sat in the car and nodded his head as the starter motor worked. 'Ah hah,' he said in satisfaction when the engine caught. He drove from the parsonage grounds, and twice fingered the heater lever to ensure it pointed to warm. The wind harrowed end of winter gardens: paper and pottles rolled like tumbleweeds in the gutter. 'Mrs Trott,' he said, so as to keep the name in his mind as he drove.

'Mrs Trott,' he was able to say without prompting when she opened the door. Mrs Trott didn't look worn down by circumstances. She had a bold face; a high, arched nose like a cheviot ewe. But her gaze was brittle, and after she had viewed the surface of the Rev. Willis, the length of him, the clerical collar, the soft gaberdine, the calmness, she looked past him and the weeds of the drive with incorrigible hope that something more than had appeared was at hand; something of extraordinary promise. The lottery man, one of the young doctors from television, the stamped, self-addressed envelope from the Dreyfus Agency of Confidential Introductions.

'Mrs Miller said you'd come,' she said. She maintained her brittle gaze upon the world, giving it every chance to respond. Life just hung its head, and the wind was unchecked. The Rev. Willis was not disconcerted. He stood on the doorstep. He felt no necessity to impose himself. He thought of the battle of the Colline Gate: not victory for Sulla and Crassus, but the heroism of the Samnites. He had for some time been considering whether a case could be made for the Colline Gate as their last chance to influence events in Italy; their last chance as a people.

'And how is your daughter, Mrs Trott,' he said.

'Elaine won't cry,' said Mrs Trott. 'She won't say much about it, but I know it's serious for her to have to come home. She always said she wouldn't come back no matter what. She never used to write or that. I never heard from her. She just turned up in a dreadful state.' Mrs Trott walked away from him without any invitation. The Rev. Willis went inside, closed the door, followed her down the worn carpet track. Elaine sat on the sofa, a heater close to her legs. Her face and legs were stained mauve, blue and yellow from mellowing bruises. Mrs Trott stood beside her, as if her daughter were an exhibit; a holiday sand castle, an entry in the puff-pastry section. She waited for the Rev. Willis's reaction. Elaine was indifferent.

'Oh Jesus,' she said. 'Mum, who's he,' but she wasn't interested in the answer.

'Your mother thought I might be able to help.'

'That's right,' said Mrs Trott, 'and it will give me a chance to clean up in here.' In an aimless way she began to take dishes from the kitchen table. Her bold features were all show and false promise of purpose. She herded the butter, milk, honey, salt, pepper, into the middle of the table ready for the next meal. The benches were used for storage rather than as work areas. Only one space by the sink remained, the rest was covered with canisters, magazines, packets with the tops dented closed, and pot plants in a state of desperate attrition.

The Rev. Willis placed a chair so that he was on the periphery of the heater's arc; Elaine spread her legs to dominate it more completely. He opened his mouth to speak to her.

'All right so I've been given a hiding,' she said.

'It's not the first,' said Rev. Willis.

'More and more as it happens.'

'How long have you been with your man, Elaine?'

'Nearly three years. He's only been hitting me much in the last few months though, hasn't he.'

'So now you're back here in your mother's home. No money, no job.'

'And no man,' said Mrs Trott from the kitchen.

'And pregnant,' said the Rev. Willis calmly, as a statement from experience, not observation.

'Thanks a lot,' said Elaine. She looked with intent at him for the first time. 'He's bloody sympathetic, this minister you brought, mum. Very full of christian sympathy, Jesus.'

The Rev. Willis smiled for the first time: a smile of a practical man. 'You want sympathy?' he said. 'Your mother offered you sympathy? You've found sympathy useful in the past?' Mrs Trott and Elaine laughed harshly; the Rev. Willis continued to smile. For a moment all three were united in a recognition of truth. The Rev. Willis managed to gain greater access to the heater, and bent towards it. L. Cornelius Sulla had a character of fascinating and baffling contradiction. As with all successful cynics there was much in his personality which attracted modern man. Only in single-mindedness did Caesar have an advantage. Sulla's strange, indulgent face was likened by a contemporary to a mulberry sprinkled with flour, and he more than most even of the Romans could mock himself. Old fierce, lazy Sulla. Old lucky Sulla; old Felix.

The Rev. Willis looked away from the bright element. 'The first thing is whether you want to go back to him,' he said.

'No,' she said. 'I'm sick of the bastard. I bled for two days the last time. The doctor said I had clots in my sinuses and all.'

'She doesn't want to go back again,' said Mrs Trott morosely.

'And I want an abortion don't I. I can't keep a kid by myself.'

'You need to contact the women's refuge centre,' he said. 'They know the procedures, both medical and legal, that can help you, and they will get in touch with the Welfare people. You see someone will have to talk to your man before he conveniently disappears.'

'I'm not making any charges or that.'

'For money; if the baby comes.' The Rev. Willis was patient. He knew that he would have to make the call himself. Mrs Trott and her daughter disliked any contact with even semi-official organizations. Forgetfulness, delay, moods, were their unrealized evasions. 'I'll ring now,' he said.

'Does it mean people coming around. More questions.'

'Or you go there.'

'But asking questions and so on.'

'You need all the help you can get,' said Mrs Trott. 'Don't you expect me to arrange everything; the kid and everything; money to support you and everything. I can't be expected to do it.'

'Well ring the refuge group then,' said Elaine. 'Ring anyone you like, if they'll help, even if they do go yack, yack, yack. I've had it. I don't care.' She turned her head away as a form of settling it;

giving permission as a favour to allow the Rev. Willis to make the call and seek assistance for her. 'Yea, why not,' she said. 'Jesus it's cold in here, mum.'

The woman at the centre was well known to the Rev. Willis. He told her the story of Elaine. 'She's been rather badly beaten, but she's over the worst. Also there's a child on the way and she will want to talk to you about that. No, because she doesn't want any police action you see.' The Rev. Willis and the refuge woman were matter of fact. Elaine sat by the heater and felt the bruises along the line of her chin. Mrs Trott rolled some scraps in newspaper, and put the parcel on the bench as the tidy-bin was full. She whistled, or rather she thought she whistled: it just missed out being a whistle and was instead a sibilance like a tuneful whisper. 'She's fortunate there,' said the Rev. Willis. 'She's able to stay with her mother here for a while.' He gave the address and phone number. 'Resources are limited you understand,' he said. Neither Mrs Trott nor her daughter were interested in his conversation.

'It's still damn sore down from the ear,' said Elaine.

'Is it,' said Mrs Trott. She felt down from her own ear, but made no other comment. The Rev. Willis finished his phone call, and came back towards them.

'Someone will come round,' he said. 'You'll find them very capable in this situation.'

'I would've gone in time. I would've gone tomorrow.' Elaine felt organization closing in on her.

'I'll visit the Welfare division on your behalf,' the minister said.

'I can't live on nothing,' Elaine said. She was abruptly and briefly sick on the floor before her, and over the heater which sizzled. 'Shit,' she said. Mrs Trott started calling out. Elaine put her hand to her mouth, and walked out of the room

Mrs Trott refused to cope. She stood by the window, became quiet, and stared boldly away at other people, other houses. The Rev. Willis took the largest pot from the bench and filled it with warm water. He used the damp tea-towel and cleaned up as best as he could. He noticed that carrot is a vegetable very resistant to digestion.

Sulla revenged himself on his enemies following the civil war: he had a long memory. His family was patrician but declined.

He needed wealth as well as power. Cicero said he plundered the rich. Sulla murdered thousands with calculation. From the slaves of those he murdered Sulla raised a special body-guard of 10,000 men, and freed them to gain their loyalty. L. Cornelius Sulla was as vicious as any when he chose.

'It's best cleaned up right away,' said the Rev. Willis. He washed his hand with detergent in the kitchen sink, then went up the hall towards the front door. 'Goodbye, Elaine,' he said as he passed the bathroom. There was no reply.

'She's got down to it lately, you see,' said Mrs Trott at the door. 'She says she's cold all the time. I can't hardly get her to wash herself, and she won't cry. Won't cry at all; she won't let herself.'

'She will need all the help you can give her for a time. Not bothering about anything, not being able to care, is part of her condition at present.'

'She never did bother much,' said Mrs Trott. 'Never did bother about me that's for sure.' She stared past the Rev. Willis with her rather vacant, bold face to see if anything exciting was happening on the neighbours' lawns, or in the cold street. Disappointed, she returned her attention to him. 'It would be nice to be able to cook a hot meal for us; meat and vegetables. We're that short you see.' The Rev. Willis put two long fingers into his coat pocket and took from it a ten dollar note folded carefully into a square scarcely larger than a stamp. He had known exactly where to find it. He smiled at Mrs Trott, who smoothed the note out in her hands.

'Later we can give her sympathy,' he said.

'Thank you for coming,' she said. 'Elaine and me might come along one Sunday; not this next one though. You know how things are at the moment.' She considered the offer to put themselves in the way of conversion was sufficient repayment. The Rev. Willis did up the top button of his soft coat, and went down the path.

'He gave me ten dollars,' said Mrs Trott to Elaine. On the way through the passage she had been wondering whether to mention it, but all her life she had passed on what information she had. Elaine was on the sofa again.

'But it's not his, is it,' she said. 'They've got a fund haven't they, and he just dishes it out from the fund. He's no loser by it don't you worry.'

'Still, ten dollars.'

'For Christ's sake,' said Elaine. She put a finger inside her mouth to check her damaged gum. 'Do you know that bastard even loosened all my teeth,' she said.

Richard Oliff was trimming the grass edges of his driveway, garden and barbecue area. He didn't have to bend, for he had a small machine on a pole which whirled a special twine and cut the grass. Oliff wished to show the Rev. Willis how it worked, and the minister obediently stood in the wind and observed. Oliff demonstrated how easily the cord could be renewed. 'It really is so convenient; so simple,' said Richard Oliff. He leant the machine on the barbecue wall of clinker brick, and took the Rev. Willis to the house for a cup of tea. 'Walter has called in to ask me to be auditor again,' he told his wife. 'Of course I will. I've been telling him that we feel we should support the church where we can.' Mrs Oliff agreed. She had a quiet voice, and a blue leisure suit for Saturday morning. She had a degree in biology and tutored part-time at the Polytech.

The Rev. Willis sat in obeisance before the fashionable pot-bellied burner which took the centre of the living room. He drank his tea. He could feel the natural warmth from the wood burner, and he undid his coat the better to receive it. 'It seems very fuel efficient,' he said.

'I got it from Mike Treddaway; general manager of Cladden Industries. Do you know him?'

'No.'

'Brother of Cecil Treddaway, the golf pro at the Heights.'

'No, I haven't met them.'

'Anyway, he gave me a very reasonable deal on two of them. One for the Wanaka place as well you see. They're being exported all over the world now you know. Quite a success. Mind you I see a fair bit of him one way and another: common organizations and so on.'

'It does use a lot of wood,' said Mrs Oliff. 'And all needing to be cut to a precise length. But it is a lovely heat.'

'You must be warm in your own home, for goodness sake,' said Oliff. He stated it as a consideration which had been carelessly overlooked too often by other people.

'How is old Mrs Preen?' said Mrs Oliff.

'I visited her on Friday. Very frail I'm afraid; very frail, and wandering a bit at times.'

'She should see Dr McKay,' said Oliff. He couldn't remember who Mrs Preen was. 'Do you know Alex McKay?'

'Only to say hello to.'

'Very astute man.'

'Ah,' said the Rev. Willis.

'A fine doctor and a personal friend. Very astute in financial matters and local administration. Oh yes.'

The Rev. Willis sat by the fashionable burner, forgetting his social responsibilities as to small talk in the pleasure of its warmth. Marius sent Sulla to King Bocchus in 105. It may well have been a trap, but Sulla loved a gamble, and had the arts of diplomacy as well as of a soldier. He persuaded Bocchus to betray his ally and come over to Rome. Marius could have wished some other outcome perhaps. Marius and Q. Caecilius Metellus were granted triumphs, but surely Marius could feel a shadow. He knew Sulla was more than a dashing commander of cavalry.

'Yes,' said Richard Oliff after a time. 'Well, I must get back out and finish the jobs in the garden before lunch. Club foursomes this afternoon. The title to defend in fact.' He waited for this to elicit some expression of interest so that he might expand on it, but the Rev. Willis said nothing.

'Would you like some more tea?' said Mrs Oliff. The Rev. Willis was struck by the whiteness and symmetry of her teeth.

'No thank you.' He recognized his cue to leave.

The Oliffs went with him as far as the barbecue. They lifted their hands. 'That old, creased coat!' said Mrs Oliff. 'Justification in itself for a larger stipend.'

'A real flasher's overcoat. He's not one for sartorial splendour, our Walter.'

'It's a calling I suppose. He's some sort of expert on the Romans. Miriam said he addressed her university extension class and bored her to distraction.' Mrs Oliff turned a little, so that she could see the wrought iron gates and the paved area before the garages. Oliff enjoyed it when his wife paid some attention to him. He prolonged the conversation.

'He's cut off from real life though, don't you think? A very insulated vocation in this day and age; put apart from others by its very nature, don't you think?' Mrs Oliff was on her way back to the house. Oliff watched her retreat, then extended a new piece of cord from his edge cutters. He began to trim the grass that grew around the trunks of his birch trees and the Irish Yews. It was a matter of some concern to him, and he gave it his full concentration.

When he returned home the Rev. Willis did not leave the garage immediately. He sat on an upturned tin which had held semi-gloss exterior, and he looked under the car to see if there was any oil dripping. Sulla's descendants found the grandeur of the name a curse. Faustus Cornelius Sulla Felix was as stupid a man as ever became consul. He married a daughter of Claudius. Nero exiled him, but even in southern Gaul the name of Sulla was too great a threat, and the Emperor's assassins came to punish him for it.

The Rev. Willis had forgotten to observe the oil patch after a time, and he was cold. He went to his study, turned on the heater, hung his soft coat on the side of the book case which reached to the ceiling. He took a ten dollar note from the shallow drawer above the knee space of his desk. He folded the ten dollars until it was not much larger than a stamp, and placed it in the pocket of his coat. On his desk calendar he wrote, check with welfare re Mrs Trott's daughter, include Oliff's acceptance as auditor in church news. He took his Sunday planning sheet to confirm the hymns he had chosen, and to revise his sermon on the relevance of personal doubt in the protestant faith. It was a sermon that he had given several times over the years.

The telephone drew him into the hall again. The Rev. Willis regarded the uneven coathooks by the stairs — ornate, old-fashioned coathooks with nothing on them. 'Don't be embarrassed at all Mrs Morrison,' said the Rev. Willis. 'A sudden bereavement is more than any of us can be expected to bear by ourselves. How long ago was this, Mrs Morrison? I'll come round right away.'

In 79 B.C. Sulla resigned his power and retired to his estates. He let them get on with it by themselves. Scipio Africanus, Caesar, Pompey, are the names heard more often, yet Sulla knew the end of the Republic. He was the first to strike coins with his own head: he had it all and gave it all away. His epitaph recorded that no friend surpassed him in kindness, and no enemy in wickedness. He died badly at the very end of course; old Sulla, old Felix.

Trumpeters

The Trumpeters were a family of very tall, very quiet farmers, who had looked down on other people over many generations — not in a patronising manner, but as if in commiseration at the mutual necessity of striking some sort of compromise with life. The Trumpeters were old inhabitants; not wealthy, but with the livelihood of their property beneath their large feet.

Their farm was in Trumpeters' Road; an indication of the family's ties with the district. An unsealed road amongst the downs, white with dust like white pollen in the summer, and a yellow pollen sign at the corner with Trumpeters' Road marked in black. It was limestone country, karst country, with sink holes and rilled limestone outcrops which were weathered grey, or showed pale yellow as a more recent skin. The larger caves had faint, attenuated Maori drawings, written over with the bolder egotism of Killjoy was here, Wanker, and Pink Floyd.

Neil Trumpeter was my age: my father had taught us both in the two room primary school. Trumpeters were not scholars, but each generation did its time patiently there, and then at the High School: purgatories completely foreign to their natures, but borne as some sort of social exaction before they had earned the right to return to their land. Old Man Trumpeter admitted that there was a need for boys to mix with others for a while. He made it sound a part of his creed of stockmanship. It was difficult however for a Trumpeter to mix — always head and shoulders above anybody else. Trumpeters were born distinct by both build and temperament. Old Man Trumpeter came to the parents' interviews and sat on a primary chair. My father would try not to smile, and the folds of Trumpeter's best trousers would envelop the little chair. Old Man Trumpeter's hands were like dragons' feet, and he laid them neatly at a distance on his knees. He never began a conversation; and in reply he spoke slowly, almost as if he were watching one word out of sight before releasing the next. His country sentences had gaps for wind and clouds to gather in, for crops to be observed, for memories to well up powerfully behind the eyes. Old Man Trumpeter advanced on to language as he would an untried bridge — with caution and reserve. 'That's about the size of it,' was his persistent idiom of concurrence.

When I was at school with Neil, his grandfather was still alive. I saw him once sitting bowed in the passenger side of the truck cab, his head framed like a Borgia engraving; and once waiting in the sun at the road gate for the rural delivery man. Age had shrunk him to almost human proportions, and his head sat directly on his shoulders: the neck retracted or the shoulders risen. The grandfather lived to be ninety-eight, but Old Man Trumpeter didn't live anything like as long, and died only a few years after his father, leaving Neil and Mrs Trumpeter alone on the property.

Neil was rather progressive for a Trumpeter. He enjoyed sport at High School and did well in the long jump and high jump. He was liked well enough — there was an absence of malice in the Trumpeter character — and his height and reserve gave him an individuality that pleased his peers. He was called Dawk; not because of anything unusual about his genitalia, but because all Trumpeters were called Dawk at the school. The nickname once coined, was passed on in a serviceable continuity. Neil failed his exams with equanimity and a sense of tradition, and returned to the property in Trumpeters' Road.

Neil and his mother were apparently quite happy to work their land together after Old Man Trumpeter died, but if it had been otherwise they would have seen it as no one's concern but their own. When Neil was in his late twenties Mrs Trumpeter died suddenly; in a hot summer, my father said, and only a few days after she and Neil had been stung by bees when they knocked a hive over with the tractor and trailer. The doctor said that it wasn't the stings that had anything to do with her dying; that it was haemorrhage of the brain, but anyway she'd barely lost the swelling from the stings when she died, and Neil told the beekeeper he wouldn't have hives on his property any more.

119

With his mother gone, Neil must have become very aware of his bachelorhood; whether for reasons of personal comfort, or the sharper realisation that he was the last Trumpeter, I can't say, but in his deliberate way he began to look for a wife. He was seen standing amidst race-goers, sports supporters, revellers, even committees. A decent, single man of property looking for a wife. He married Tessa Hall within a year. She was a librarian, and quite new to town. She wasn't at all what you'd expect of a librarian, for Tessa was glowing, chatty, impulsive. She sang parts in the local repertory, and entered the Floral Princess competition — and won. Other men envied Trumpeter his wife's looks, and other women endorsed Tessa's wisdom in annexing security. She wasn't tall; but then the height of Trumpeter women had never affected the inexorable gene that persisted through the male line.

I imagine that the routine and isolation of farm life were something of a shock for Tessa Trumpeter. People were the world as far as she was concerned, and the chaffinch flocks above the crops, easterly drizzle caressing the downs, thick flight of grass grub in the night, dark lucerne in the evening light: what could she make of it? And they were drought years, which while not really threatening a debt free and established farm like Trumpeters' nevertheless meant that there wasn't money for shopping trips to Auckland or major renovations of the farmhouse. I did hear someone say that the marriage was in trouble early on, but you hear that about most marriages at some time; maybe with truth.

Neil sold out after about five years of marriage. He and Tessa moved to town, and Neil bought motels on the main road — the Shangri-la Lodge Motels. Neil joined Lions, and had his photo in the paper several times with a salmon on opening day. Tessa did most of the work at the motel, and the bustle of people, new and familiar, suited her. They were a popular couple. I saw them occasionally on the modest social round of a country town: once or twice at their own place, with Neil standing above his barbecue guests with an expectant smile, even when it was over. Who can say concerning the happiness of others; the greater part of our life is wasted in pretence of one sort or another.

Yet by chance alone I know something of how it worked out for Neil Trumpeter. I had been staying the weekend with my parents in the schoolhouse, and I went running in the evening — part of a forlorn effort to stave off middle age. The privacy of the country saved me from the derision of town acquaintances. The dust of Trumpeters' Road puffed out beneath my feet as I jogged in the late amber light. I kept to an easy pace, and had time enough to watch the car and tall figure on the roadside. There is a point on Trumpeters' Road, high on the downs, which gives a good view over much of the Trumpeter place and adjoining properties. You can look down and see the thick, Oamaru stone posts at the entrance, the track from the road gate, the farmhouse and outbuildings, the creek course marked with rough growth in the hills. I could see all that: I could see the abandoned machinery in the grass behind the equipment shed, a record of the Trumpeters' modest technological advance over several generations. Each piece of machinery cannibalized of useful parts, and left just thick tines, flaps, rods and springs in a clenched frenzy of rust. Neil Trumpeter could see it all as well. He had a casual shirt in the fashionable fitting cut, and blue with contrasting white collar and cuffs; yet I could sense the indifference to what he wore, so typical of a Trumpeter. His plain face was clean shaven, with just a patch of thick hairs on each cheek above the shaving line. I stopped beside him and had a spell. It is always difficult to avoid feeling small and fussy beside a Trumpeter. 'Looking at the old place, Neil,' I said, and watched the birches at the road gate and the lengthening shadows amongst the downs.

'That's about the size of it,' he said. He had one hand over the head of a wooden fence post as if it were struggling to leave the ground.

'Do you see much of the people who have it now?' I said. Neil didn't answer. From his quiet height he gazed over the farm he knew. There was a sense of enquiry in his look, as if he wished some response from the place itself. He looked on the lost land that slow Trumpeter voices had sounded over for a hundred years.

'Sweet, sweet Jesus,' he said. 'What have I done.'

A Day
With Yesterman

Chatterton woke to the birds. The absence of pain may have been the reason. He moved his legs, sucked in his stomach, but nothing caught; just the squeak of the plastic sheet beneath the cotton one. Chatterton was accustomed to the need to occupy himself much of the night; to sidle and belay from ledge to ledge of darkness, but not all that often did he hear the birds begin. He marvelled at the intensity — a sweet hubbub as a base, and superimposed the longer, individual exclamations of thrush or blackbird. He had the pleasing thought that the birds gathered at his house to inaugurate a special day. Chatterton folded the sheet under his chin, so that the blanket no longer tickled, and he made himself a little wider and longer to pop a few joints and check that he was in good shape.

A mild suffusion of light from behind the curtains strengthened as Chatterton sang 'Danny Boy' and 'The White Cliffs of Dover'. He stopped with a feeling something of value was slipping away, and then it came to him, a recollection of the night's dream in which he had made love to an ample woman beneath an elm tree in Hagley Park. It was to some degree an explanation of his mood. Chatterton was sensible enough to enjoy authentic emotion however it reached the mind. Before the experience quite faded he closed his eyes to breathe again the fragrance of the elm and observe a wisp of auburn hair quiver with the pulse of her neck. He lay listening to his birds as morning came. How young at last I feel, he assured himself.

By the time Chatterton was in the kitchen, he could get by with natural light. He poached himself an egg without boiling off the white, and he watched his yellow feet like flounders on the floor. He would never recognise his feet in a crowd, for they were just any old, yellow feet. Truck rigs passed with a roar on the nearby motorway as they tried to get a clear start to the day. Chatterton rubbed his knee to loosen the joint. The skin seemed to have no attachment to the bones, and slid all ways. Only the young body savours its union.

As the birds wound down, Chatterton finished his third cup of tea, and went back to his bedroom to choose his clothes. 'I'll make a bargain with you.' He addressed a small, familiar god. 'Best clothes for best day.' The trousers were a quality check, but big at his waist and so the band tucked somewhat under his belt. A grey jacket, with a chrome zip, that his daughter had given him for Christmas. Tropic Sands aftershave, which the label exhorted Chatterton to splash on liberally, but which he did not. 'Chatterton,' said Chatterton to his own reflection, 'you are an old dog.' He looked at all the bottles on his drawers, and decided to take no medication at all. Before he left the house Chatterton buffed the toes of his shoes with the socks he was putting out to wash. He should have known better, for the bending sent him dizzy, and he over-balanced and fell on to the smooth lino by the bench. He had a laugh at himself, and felt the cool lino on his cheek as he lay and waited for his head to clear. In the corner was a false cut in the lino: Chatterton could remember clearly the wet day seventeen years before when he had laid the lino and made just that false cut. How difficult it is to fault life's continuity. The rain had caught the window at an angle, and drained like rubber tree striations across its surface.

As Chatterton walked to Associated Motors he calculated a route which would keep him on the sunny side of the streets, and he watched other people on their way to work, disappointed that he couldn't recognise them as friends. He nodded and smiled nevertheless.

Chatterton helped part-time with the accounts at Associated Motors; so very part-time over the last months that Susan was surprised to see him. 'And you're looking so smart today,' she said. Chatterton knew he was. He began to use the computer to calculate GST payments. Chatterton enjoyed the computer, and was impatient with people who claimed they couldn't adapt to them.

'Life is adaptation,' he said.

'Right, Mr Chatterton.'

'How I could run when I was young.'

'Could you?' said Susan.

'I was a small-town champion,' said Chatterton, 'and could have been a large-town one with training.' He was wistful rather than proud.

'I like netball,' said Susan.

'Ah, your knees are wonderfully smooth,' said Chatterton: his fingers nimble on the keys.

The Sales Manager broke up their flirtation. 'How are you feeling?' he asked.

'I am in complete remission today,' said Chatterton. 'I can sense my prime again. I'm growing young again very rapidly.' The Sales Manager laughed, for he thought Chatterton intended a joke.

'How about taking a Cressida down to Dunedin then for me. It's needed there today,' he asked Chatterton.

The mechanics watched in envy as Chatterton took a set of provisional plates and two of his own cassettes. They hoped for such perks themselves. 'Hey, Chatters, you lucky old bastard,' and Chatterton winked and executed a no-fuss manoeuvre before them in the yard.

'I thought the old bastard was dying or something.'

'Dying to get away in that car, all right.'

In fifth gear the Cressida was only loping on the Canterbury Plains. Chatterton fed in his Delius cassette and the quiet interior was sprung with sound. Chatterton wondered why he dreamed so often in old age of hang-gliding. Something he'd never done, yet increasingly his night views were from above, the cold air whistling in a rigging he didn't understand. Progress was relentless, and from landscape and people half-recognised he was borne away. He supposed it might be a side effect of the medication. When he was younger he would have tackled hang-gliding. He had been an athlete hadn't he, and a soldier?

At Karitane Chatterton turned off to take the old road. He could avoid the increasing traffic. He liked that swamp flat: rushes, brown and yellow mosses, mallards, and pukekos with their bookish, striding way. Later there was a stranded man — enquiring face and car bonnet raised. Chatterton stopped, and the man came with grateful haste to meet him. His name was Norman Caan. He began to thank Chatterton, who smiled, but was distracted by the peace as he stood there — the quiet road, the crimped blue light over the sea, the headland beyond with an apron of gorse on the steeper ground. The wind from the sea was wine, and it scented the beachside grass and bore spaciousness inland.

'I do appreciate you stopping. I've got something of a problem as you see, and I've a city appointment at one.' Caan was close to Chatterton; his voice a trifle plaintive. He put out his hand and Chatterton shook it.

'Sorry,' said Chatterton, 'but what a day it is. Isn't it? How things continue to fit newly together, year after year.'

'I suppose it is.' Caan looked at the sky, blown almost clear, and the hills and the inlet and the horizon seaward, as though he had just entered a large building and had its architecture commended to him. The coast curved, and a far cutting bore a drape of pink ice-plant, and the sun shone back from it as if from glass.

As they examined the engine of Caan's Volvo, Chatterton noticed a balding spot at Caan's crown, as if a tidy bird had been scratching a nest there. Chatterton passed a hand over his own stiff, grey hair. A dunny brush he'd heard it called. He had to admit Caan's clothes better than his own however; an integration of style and texture which Chatterton could recognise, yet not explain.

'There's nothing we can do,' said Chatterton. 'Lock up and come with me. We can have someone out in no time.' But back at his own car, instead of getting inside, Chatterton was drawn to the bank again. 'Will you look at that though,' he said. 'No pain there at all. Will you look at the ripples on the bars as the tide comes in, and the bubbles over the crab holes in the mud.' The single cloud against powder blue made a cameo brooch of the sky; birch leaves tossed as a mane on the back of a macrocarpa hedge. 'You don't mind just for a moment?' asked Chatterton. 'It's just such a day.'

'No, no,' said Caan.

'It's just such a day,' said Chatterton. Caan had no option, but his face had initially a shrug of the shoulders expression as he watched Chatterton move to the edge of the bank above the coast. He was only a few feet above the sea, yet Chatterton sucked several breaths as a diver would on a high cliff. 'I shall become part of it. I see it all as if I'm twenty,' he said.

Despite concern for his situation, Caan was affected by Chatterton's wonder, and something more — something naive in his cheerful age and the trousers belted too large, and his hair bristling. 'It is rather splendid,' said Caan; diffident in praise of his own country.

'You know,' said Chatterton, 'today I keep thinking of when I was young.'

Somewhere between Lake Grasmere and Seddon the black AJS left the road at speed and took an angle into grass standing high as a field of wheat. There was no way of stopping quickly. The bike's metal scything through. He heard only one sound, that of the rushing grass, and he was aware in the clarity of fear how bright the sun shone on that roadside grass like wheat. Yet there was nothing hidden; no snare, no ditch, and fear gave place to exultation as the grass slowed him and he KNEW that nothing there had harm in it: an instant almost too brief to allow him the dangerous conviction that he couldn't die. The black, heavy AJS off the road; the hissing, even fluster of the wheat-grass in the vivid sun. All in a few seconds, he supposed. All happening in a few seconds and in heightened perception. And the bike had stopped and he found himself quite alone in that landscape, stalled high from the road with grass packed around him, the cicadas coming back to chorus, and fine pollens settling on the black tank of the AJS.

'Like riding through a wheat field,' said Chatterton.

'Sorry?'

'I was thinking back,' said Chatterton. 'Other days.'

As they passed over the hills into the city, Chatterton and Caan, together completely by chance they would suppose, talked freely. Chatterton found it easier to be honest as he grew older, and the knowledge that relationships had no necessary continuation ceased to disconcert him. Besides, Caan was prepared to listen as well as talk. Chatterton liked a positive listener; he could be one himself. They covered the decline of state medicine, the loss of flavour in

Bluff oysters, the self-serving of the political powerful, and the suicide of Tony Hancock. There is a good deal of satisfaction to be had from free-ranging criticism. 'But then I'm a deal older than you,' said Chatterton.

'Not so much surely; I'm retired.'

'There are two possibilities as you get old,' said Chatterton. 'You become archaic, or you leave the world behind in your progress. Either way increasing isolation is the result.'

'Well, isolated numerically perhaps.'

'And in confidence. It's hard to be confident and old. The opposite of what most people expect I suppose.'

'But you are,' said Caan.

'An act of faith. Besides, superstition and disease have me now, so I indulge myself. There's days sometimes that favour you, you know.'

'Propitious,' said Caan.

'Pardon.'

'Propitious.'

'Yes,' said Chatterton. 'That's it.'

'Anyway today you're welcome to travel back with me, and have lunch with me too. I'm allowed a guest at the Rotary Lunch I'm addressing. I'll have my car delivered, and afterwards we'll pick up my sister who's coming back with me to recuperate for a while.' Caan was pleased to be able to establish the immediate future, and to provide for Chatterton's repayment within it.

The President of Rotary was a splendid host, just one size larger and more glossy than his fellows as befitted his office. 'So much of what service groups do now is taken for granted,' he said. 'Assistance is an expectation now; almost a right.' Chatterton noticed the barman's black reefer jacket, and it produced before Chatterton his grandmother's sewing basket. The fine wicker-work and the embroidered top — black, black, with a country spire perpetually slate blue. The colours were ribbed, and the tranquillity of even execution rather than the subject had made an ache which allowed of no expression. So he had built childlike barricades of pins around the black field's spire in attempts at the protection which his memory was later able to assume.

'We get told who we should be supporting, and how much,' said the President. 'We get told we're not doing enough rather than thanked. Not coughing up sufficiently.' Chatterton enjoyed a free whisky, and watched the last members picking up their badges. The President led the way into the dining room, and they took their places before three slices of ham on each plate. Chatterton rather enjoyed the Rotarian mood; an aura of confidence and good intent that arises from reasonable success in the world and a wisely unexamined life. Chatterton looked with favour on his ham, and waited for the vegetables. Caan talked to the President.

'I ran my own business for twenty-seven years, then it grew too complex and I sold out. That's one of the things I want to mention in my address: the need to understand there's a point at which a business becomes too much for the managerial skills of its founder alone. A lot of concerns go wrong at that stage.'

Chatterton admired the Rotarians across from him, particularly an assured man in his thirties, eating carefully and smiling carefully as he listened to his neighbour. A man well carapaced in a three-piece suit, and trusting the ground beneath his feet. Chatterton wondered if he himself at any age had looked that way; and knew the answer. The man had a sheen almost; the beauty of a live lobster, an exoskeleton creature, any vulnerability safe within. He was all jointed precision of appearance. Chatterton caught his eye.

'Good on you,' said Chatterton, and they lifted their forks in mutual salutation.

'Few business men can make the transition from personal to corporate management,' said Caan. 'And why should it be expected, or easy.' Caan stopped, and looked first at the President and then at Chatterton as if some explanation was expected from them. His face was pale, and he swallowed several times. 'I feel rotten,' he said. 'I think I might be sick.' His head gave a shiver, and he sighed as if lonely.

'Perhaps the cold meat,' said the President. Caan and he left the table and went through the conversations to find a place for Caan to lie down. Caan walked as if he were carrying a tray of marbles and the loss of any of them would be his death.

Chatterton was offered more vegetables, and accepted all but the peas. Sprouts he had, and potato balls and corn heaped like nuggets of gold. And no pain was swallowed with them; no pain whatsoever. The President returned alone. 'He's lying down,' he said. 'He says he feels a little better.' The President looked searchingly at Chatterton. Chatterton lacked an executive mien, and there was grey hair tufted in his ears. He alone in the dining room had a jacket with a zip. There was a sense of ease though, and good-will and self-will. The President was not a fool. 'Caan suggested you might speak instead,' he said. Chatterton was happy to be of service; he liked to talk to people. And he had his best trousers on, even if they were gathered at the waist somewhat. He had visions to draw upon, his life among them.

When the President's routine business was over and the Serjeant-at-Arms had imposed fines with sufficient humorous innuendo, Chatterton was introduced as a colleague of Norman Caan. As he waited to speak, as the polite applause eddied about the tables, Chatterton was reminded of his last Battalion reunion, and by another step of recollection Birdy Fowler, who died of heatstroke before they came out of the desert. Chatterton hadn't been invited to speak at the reunion, and he thought there was a need for Birdy's name to be heard again. So Chatterton began his talk with several of the stories Birdy used to tell when drinking: the Rotarians laughed at the ribaldry of natural man, and Chatterton laughed in tribute to a friend. Then Chatterton talked about his illness; the prostate and spleen which had been taken, the disaffection of other organs; about how to make it through the nights, the spiritual and practical ingenuities by which it's possible to inch closer to the day. About his wife who had been very beautiful when she was young and he was a coarse, stupid boy. About his dream of steam trains ascending steep tracks through the bush, so that the engine fumed and panted, the white steam like egret's feathers flared against the leaves, wild cattle crashed away, and deep, faded varnish of the inner woodwork still showed a living grain.

The green, sashed curtains quivered at the windows of the hotel. The long tables of Rotary luncheon had flower vases, and pollen beneath some of them was spread like pepper on the white cloth. A waitress with her hair up in gel was at the kitchen swing doors, ready to clear away. She picked her lip, and wondered if she would be through by four. We make the mistake of assuming that our present experience is the world's. The tussock would be blowing on all the crests of Dansey's Pass, glue sniffers sitting with statues of the city fathers, a fine rain flaking on to the pungas of the Ureweras, a sheer excalibur of sunlight from the high window of a panel shop in Papanui transfixing young Marty working there.

The Rotarians were normally uncomfortable with personal revelations, which could easily obscure sound business practices, but as Chatterton was unknown to them they felt none of the embarrassment that acquaintanceship would have brought. They were quite struck by his eccentricity, his passion, and the evident movement of the bones in his thin cheeks as he talked. Chatterton had an innocent pride as he left with the President to find Caan. He was resting on an alcove chair in the foyer. His coat and tie were off, and his head relaxed backwards. 'I think I'm all right now,' he said.

'Well, Mr Chatterton was a considerable success,' said the President.

'That's the second time he's saved the day,' said Caan.

'I just sang for my supper,' said Chatterton. The President's laugh was high-pitched; almost a giggle, and odd from such an imposing man.

Caan's car was delivered as he and Chatterton sat peacefully in the foyer. Caan washed his face with cold water, and then decided that he was recovered. 'You'll understand that Joan's had a hard time of it,' he said when he returned. 'She left her husband to make a mid-life career for herself in physiotherapy and then found she had cancer. The treatment's knocked her pretty badly.' Chatterton knew the treatment, but he didn't think about it as they drove to the nursing home. Instead he enjoyed the dappled shadows on the road through the green belt, the shimmer caused by the breeze on the tops of the trees, and imagined himself joining in with the afternoon joggers — putting his weight well forward on the slope and judging a pace to keep both legs and lungs comfortable. The bellows of the chest in full use; cooling tree air on the damp singlet; hair heavy with sweat patting on the back of his head as he ran.

On the front lawn of the nursing home a badminton court had been marked out. Young people played vigorously there, their bare feet silent on the grass, their voices loud and sudden. Joan was waiting in the lounge with her two cases beside her. 'She'll need a good deal of rest of course, but we're all optimistic,' Caan said as he and Chatterton walked past the lawn. Chatterton watched a brown girl leap forever so that her arms and breast were outlined against the sea. He wondered why God still chose to punish old men. As Caan came closer to the lounge he smiled and raised his hand, but his sister was behind the glass, and nothing could be said. She wore a light dress of floral pattern that would be considered cheerful perhaps — when purchased for someone else. She wore lipstick but her eyebrows were very pale, and to hide her baldness she was topped with a tam-o-shanter, green and red. She had the eyes of the travellers of illness.

'I'm sorry we're a bit late,' said Caan. 'It's been an odd sort of day.' As he told her of it, and Chatterton's part as an explanation for his presence, Joan and Chatterton regarded one another. When Caan finished, Chatterton touched the woollen cap in a friendly way.

'I had a hat, but not as colourful as yours,' he said. He took one of her cases, Caan the other, and they waited at the door while Joan farewelled a nurse. 'Chemotherapy as well as the ray can be pretty much a sapping combination,' said Chatterton when she was back. 'Is your hair all out?'

'All out,' she said.

'So was mine,' said Chatterton, 'but it grows in again. Mine grew back very wiry.'

'Very wiry,' said Joan. Well, frankness could work both ways.

'And you get a good deal of strength back.' To demonstrate, Chatterton stopped by the car and threw the case up, and caught it again in both arms. 'See,' he said eagerly.

'You get used to him,' said Caan.

'Are you so very different?' she asked Chatterton.

'I'm in search of natural man now,' he said.

'Too late, too old,' she said, but Chatterton threw up the case again and capered with it. The badminton players cheered; a nurse stood watching from the office and telling others over her shoulder what was happening.

Caan asked Chatterton to drive. After his illness at lunch Caan wanted a restful trip. Chatterton was obliging once more. As he drove he calculated aloud the unexpected profit he was making on the day — the price of the bus fare to Christchurch, and of a midday meal. Enough for a week's groceries, or for semi-gloss to paint his small porch. 'Do you enjoy painting?' he asked Joan. The triviality of it stimulated Joan; she was tired of weighing up life and death. She began to talk of the renovations she had done years before on her house at Port Chalmers. Although her voice was well back in her throat, and somewhat husky, it increased in tempo and her tam-o-shanter nodded green and red. 'Oh, no, no,' interrupted Chatterton decidedly. 'You should always strip back before repapering for a first rate job.'

'It's not always needed.'

'Shoddy, shoddy,' cried Chatterton.

'What would a man know about making a home,' said Joan. 'What does a man remember.'

Chatterton was in the presence of things which gave an answer. The water in the pink heart of flax, and a monkey puzzle tree to hold up the sky. Sheep coughing out the night, and in a winter drizzle the horses smoking in the dray. His mother standing at the laundry, pushing back her hair with her wrist, smiling at him, and the smell of hot woollens and yellow soap again. Old coats without shoulders on nails there like dried fish, and gulls following his father's plough.

At Timaru they had cream freezes, and turned off from the main road at the Showground Hill to rest and eat. Chatterton leant his arms on the top wire of the fence, and watched the downs and the mountains beyond. He led a game to distinguish as many shades of green as possible. 'Nine different colours. To stand and see nine different colours of green,' said Joan. 'All growing from the same soil; all compatible and with the promise of some use or crop.'

When he looked south, Chatterton sensed a change in the weather, and he told the others to expect a southerly. A fisherman gets to read the elements of his locality. Chatterton encouraged Joan to talk as they went on north. He refused to be deferential just because of her trial. 'You have to be careful illness doesn't make you selfish, you know,' he said. 'And you could do a lot more with your appearance — a young woman like you.' He could say such things because of his own illness, his lack of malice, but mostly because of a special innocence which arises from experience and is the mark of rare and successful old age.

'I was never at all religious before,' said Joan. 'Now I'm an atheist by faith rather than logic. And I've got tired of most of my friends: they almost bored me to death when they came. What you expect rarely happens. You, Norman, you're one of the worst.'

'But I'm a brother. All brothers are boring. They lack sufficient biological variation to be otherwise.'

Eventually release was almost overpowering for Joan. 'It's stuffy,' she said. 'I feel dizzy.'

'It's the closeness before the change,' said Caan, 'and you're not used to travelling yet.' Joan took off her woollen hat, and leant back on the seat. Her naked, bird's head had a little downy hair, and the skull plates joined in apparently clumsy workmanship.

'The treatment can have a long term effect on your food preferences,' said Chatterton. 'Peas and beans for instance. I can't eat them at all now; the smell disgusts me, while fruit is a positive craving. Nectarines and satsumas: ah, there now.'

The southerly came through late in the afternoon, catching them before Ashburton. The churned cloud, wind that flogged the trees and bore a scattered rain too pressed to set in. The temperature dropped as if a door had been opened. 'Oh, that's much better,' said Joan.

'Let's sing "Danny Boy". You know "Danny Boy"?' said Chatterton.

'Oh Danny Boy, the pipes — — —.' Three of them together. Chatterton likes to sing, although he has a poor voice. He watched the broad, shingle river bed, the islands of gorse and lupin in the scattered rain. He thought of his nineteen pound salmon near the mouth of the Waitaki; the gravel unsure beneath his waders as he turned, and the cry going up from his fellow fishermen as they gave way for him. The salmon don't feed: they strike in anger or home-coming exultation perhaps. The river aids its fish against the line, and swans form a necklace above the struggle as they pass to Lake Wainoni.

'We're all a bit high,' said Joan. 'I like the song, but we've all light voices and we need someone deeper. A bass baritone, say.' The southerly was blowing itself out, but the coolness remained. Near Dunsandel they saw a hitchhiker with a giant pack and the legs to make light of it. Chatterton pulled up ahead of him.

'Can you sing "Danny Boy"?' he asked. The hitchhiker was willing, although for a time he was embarrassed by Joan's head.

'Where do you come from?' she said.

'Dubbo, Australia.'

'We've all of us got problems,' said Caan.

There were enough voices for a barbershop quartet. 'Oh Danny Boy, the pipes — —.' The Australian sang well. He was out of the weather and travelling in the right direction. Over the sinews of his brown arms were raised a few graceful arteries, and the whites of his eyes glinted in a tanned face. 'The green, green grass of home — —' they sang as Caan conducted. Joan and the hitchhiker, who couldn't remember each other's names and would never meet again, combined their voices, and smiled at each other because of Chatterton's caterwauling.

They dropped the Australian baritone at the city overbridge. Chatterton took his pack from the boot, and Joan gave him a bag of seedless grapes she had from the nursing home. 'Goodbye Danny Boy,' she said. What could he make of them: what could they make of themselves. A hitchhiker's experience is only life accelerated. 'Oh my God,' said Joan as they went on. 'I've had my hat off all that time. What a sight.' She laughed at her own humiliation, and wiped her eyes. She put the tam-o-shanter on once more, for the formality of parting with Chatterton.

The wooden house was like the others that surrounded it; insufficiently individual it seemed to be his. Chatterton stood in the drive as Caan came round to take the driver's seat. The evening was calm, but the evidence of the southerly was there. Leaves stripped by the wind and gathered on the concrete in the lee of the house. Leaves of peach and maple. Leaves of birch with aphids still clustered on the underside. The wind's violence had in its eddy a delicacy of graduated winnowing, and the litter diminished to a whip tail of fragments which included two ladybirds, a length of tooth floss, tuft of cat fur, and ended in a line of most fragile, perfect dust.

'But we'll keep in touch,' Caan was saying. 'You cheer Joan up because you know what she's been through, and she won't have many people to visit her while she's here.'

'If you can be bothered some time,' said Joan. The sheen of her hospital skin wrinkled in a grin.

'You know, right from the very start I had a feeling this was going to be a good day,' said Chatterton. 'It's a sort of Indian summer perhaps.'

'Life is sad though, isn't it?' said Joan. She looked up at him with a terrible openness.

'Oh yes, sad, but not dreary, not lacking purpose. But sad sure enough,' said Chatterton firmly. He went to the protected corner of his small garden and came back with a red rose for Joan; an old English rose, dark and red. 'Old style roses have the true scent,' he said. 'Aren't I right.' She had it to her face. 'Eh?' he said.

'Yes.'

Two white butterflies tumbled in the air above the letter box, and Chatterton smiled, not withdrawing his attention from the car as Caan backed out. 'He's a hard case that one,' said Caan. 'He gave a speech off the cuff at the Rotary meeting you know. Hardly a moment for thought.'

'He's certainly got no singing voice, but he sees through things all right.'

Chatterton waited to see them drive away; not the last minute shame-faced turning of some people's farewells, as if they feared what might be being said of them. Only his trousers suggested age; crimped at his slender waist and bagging somewhat at the seat the way trousers of old men do. When they were gone Chatterton arched back cautiously, and pressed with the flat of his hand on his stomach. He decided to stay in his garden while he felt so well. Did he tell them he was an athlete once, he wondered. Unthinkingly he kept his arched stance as he tried to remember. All the things he could do then, all the things he could feel. Chatterton could see his dark roses on the fence, and the two ladybirds upside down and closer in the whip tail dust upon the concrete.

The scent of the rose seemed to linger, maybe only in his heart, for he was no longer sure of such distinctions. What would he think of next, he wondered. He would fetch a beer and have it in his garden, because of the extra money and the friends he had made that day. As he turned to go, he had in recollection the sight of the Marlborough hills, and a hawk the colour of a moth against the sea of the sky.

Essie

Dan had been offered a hotel lunch: three courses and more talk of business when all that was necessary had been said. He could have lunched in any of the Mall cafeterias, with used dishes pushed to the end of the tables and the clatter of plastic trays like a mechanical language around him. Instead he sat on a green bench beneath the trees on the bank of the river. He had a carton of fruit juice and a cheese sandwich; he watched the seagulls and mallards begging scraps from the people on the grass, and in the shallow river the soft weed imitate the motion of fish. The vehicles of the one-way systems pursued each other on both sides of the park, but the lawns and the path close to the water were in the bright sun, and the seats beneath the trees in dappled warmth, and the oaks and sycamores deflected the noise. Ducks sought out the acorns which were like copper bullets, and amazingly swallowed them whole. Seagulls couldn't, and they hunched their shoulders and shrieked. There were leaves floating on the water, turning as they went as if to show themselves to advantage, and others had sunk in the calmest places and lay on the bottom as massed, dark prints of a hand.

Dan saw the girls in their summer dresses and young office men with neat hair and their jackets off. And a group of uniformed N.C.O.s from the Army Hall, who were office workers also and had escaped from their proformas to the grass and the sun. The girls in their summer dresses seemed the same as those he remembered from his time in the city: the same sharp eyebrows and vulnerable throats; the same aura, in those who were alone, of absorption and resistance to the glance, that he recalled single girls in the park to always have.

136

Each time the lights changed there was a roar from the traffic zoo, but the greater the competition there, the more tranquil was the riverside, and the clearer and more deliberate the movement and colours. The seagulls hunched with their red beaks open in a call, the leaves as slow Catherine wheels on the surface of the river, and the girls with their books and lunches open on the grass.

He didn't recognise Essie at first. The woman came with her son in a push-chair, and sat on the stone steps of the fountain. She lifted the boy from the chair, and he splashed in the water with his hands, and ran a few paces to one side then the other. She was compact and calm, and wore a white, lace blouse. Only later, when Dan had been watching the river, and glanced up when she stood, did he see that it was Essie. He felt a flow of pleasure and affection; then an ebb of regret. He smiled, although at that distance and amongst the various people on the grass and seats, Essie had no idea that he was there. It was an involuntary smile, marking at once the recollection and recognition of Essie. 'It's Essie,' he heard himself say quietly. Essie's boy ran back from the ducks, and Essie picked him up and went towards the ducks to show there was nothing to fear. The sun loaded the air so that it was resistant to movement, and direct reflections were difficult to bear. Some people had been pressed flat on to the grass, and lay with their arms spread out in surrender.

Essie sat back on the steps, her white blouse vivid against the stones. It was appropriate, he thought, that Essie should have fountains behind her, and further the river. The fountain was not at all spectacular. The jets were unchanging, but the streams reached their undramatic height and came apart, glittered and fell. Essie and he had spent a life it seemed by the sea, rivers and swimming baths: for much of that time Dan had watched, as he watched once more, Essie as the focus of the action.

His Essie. Essie dives again; again. One unhurried exercise in technique after another, and then perhaps the coach has a few words to say, lifting the palms of his hands in exposition as he gives his advice. Essie doesn't care if Dan is there, or if he comes at the end of the practice. One bounce on the board for lift; her thigh muscles block for a moment, and she arcs and twists in the air above the water. Afterwards while she is changing, Dan remains almost alone on the tiered seating. A few other swimmers practice, but Essie's repetition seems to have perpetuated her image above the pool, and Dan sees her continue to arch and dive: her dark costume firm, and her legs aligned.

They walk back together to her house. Essie dressed has almost a chunky look — handsome rather than glamorous. Dan makes her laugh by exaggerating the events and personalities of the office where he works, and takes advantage to press and kiss her before he leaves. Essie closes her eyes as if the intimacy is too much for her to witness or to bear, and Dan sees her dark lashes, and the lids sensitive and trembling over her eyes. She has brown, sleek skin, and a space between her front teeth. As he kisses her, even as he sees her face and feels her body, he has again the image of Essie diving. Essie by herself, concentrating on herself: the heavy rattle of the diving board, and Essie compact and quick in the air.

Dan wondered if observation of Essie was enough, the conjuror for memories of Essie and himself. To watch at a distance and recollect suited his mood and posed no contradiction to his version of the past. Yet it seemed furtive to give no sign; to turn away from Essie seen in the summer park and say nothing. He walked along the path by the river, and then across the worn grass to the fountain, and saw Essie stand to meet him. The reaction that he felt, the quick charge of odd emotion, was not for her voice, though it was much the same, but for the recognition of what was familiar in her presence in relation to his own as they stood there: the precise angle of her face up to his, the physical, spatial relationship repeated and reaffirmed after many years. It caused in him a brief malaise even as they talked and sat down on the steps together; a shadow part tenderness, part sorrow, the malaise of mortality acknowledged which accompanies such reunions. 'Yes, I've been watching you from the seats beneath the trees,' he said. Essie told him they often came to the river after they'd been shopping.

'I saw you once in Nelson, at Christmas time,' she said, 'with your family at the carnival. We were on the Big Wheel, at the top waiting for all the seats to fill. I could see right round, and you were with your wife and daughter, going down towards the sea.

'Do you still dive at all,' said Dan.

'Not for years. God, no. I go sometimes to the swim fit classes at the main pool. That's all now.'

'Diving was so much the thing with you. In a way I was jealous of it once I suppose.'

'It's a young person's sport, like so many these days. I gave up years ago.' Yet Essie still seemed young. Her wrists were strong, and her shoulders well developed from the swimming. Her hair shone in the sun. But a calm Essie; so different from the changeable, sudden Essie he had known. The new Essie was at ease with herself and others. She could talk with him, or let the talk trail away without care, so that they were left to enjoy their joint presence and the languor of the riverside.

The office workers began to leave; the girls in their summer dresses, the young men in shirt-sleeves with watches glinting on their wrists, army N.C.O.s in jungle green. They moved reluctantly away from the paths, the oaks, the river. The traffic zoo roared; the city took them.

'I'll have to get Richard home. He'll become grumpy if he doesn't have his meal.'

'Of course,' said Dan.

'Have you got time to come back with us for a while? If you're not picking up your daughter until the shops shut, why don't you?' Dan considered refusing, not because he wanted to leave Essie, not because he might be imposing, but from a trivial pride that he'd have to admit that he'd planned no significant alternative: no meetings on property matters, or promised visits to friends.

'I was just going to sit here, then perhaps have a drink in a hotel,' he said. 'I haven't got any other business. I'm just the chauffeur waiting until required.'

'I have both sun and alcohol at my place.'

Dan took the push-chair, Essie held Richard by the hand, and as a small family they walked through the trees to the carpark. 'I'm not used to having an afternoon off in the week,' said Dan. 'It seems more than just coincidence that I should happen to come up today and you be here. Things have chosen to catch up.'

'It's not so odd to me. I live here; I'm quite often in the park with Richard in the summer, after shopping.'

'I still feel a sense of intention.'

'Once things have happened it's easy to think them inevitable,' said Essie. 'If you'd met some other friend you'd think just the same.'

'Maybe,' said Dan. He folded the push-chair and put it in the boot of Essie's car, and in his own car he followed her; first through the busy city and then into the suburbs which were quiet, and where the intense sun made sharp, Spanish shadows.

Essie led him into walled privacy at the back of the house: grass and trees, and deck chairs around a sand pit. The striped canvas of the chairs had been bleached almost white, and was warm to Dan's touch. He was left there with a glass of red wine while Essie gave Richard his lunch. 'Go to sleep if you like,' said Essie. 'I won't be long.' Essie had a large house, but it was obvious she and her husband weren't gardeners. The lawn was kept down by drought rather than cutting, and tufted edges merged with an overgrown garden. Bright berries on currant bushes winked in the sun, and tall grass fringed the trunks of fruit trees. It was a garden which spoke of live and let live; of an absence of zealotry.

Essie filled his glass again when she came out. 'Comfortable?' she said.

'Except for my feet.' The heat of the city and the unyielding pavements had made his feet sweat and ache. Essie pointed out a tap at the edge of the lawn, almost hidden by the currant bushes, and Dan took off his shoes and socks, and washed his feet there.

'I'm afraid we're not much as gardeners,' called Essie without apology. 'We let the plants fight it out amongst themselves.'

'Laissez faire,' said Dan.

'What.'

'Nothing.' The dry grass of the lawn was disconcerting under his bare feet as he came back. 'Laissez faire,' he said, and walked through the sand pit for the novelty of its texture.

'Bare-foot boy again,' said Essie.

Apples were the only fruit that Dan could see on any of the trees; small apples, most with blemishes, for nothing was pruned or sprayed. One large golden elm stood by the gate. None of its leaves had fallen. They were flat leaves; extravagant crepe yellow extended against the wall and the sky. Essie talked of things and people they had known together. He recognized them, though each had an oddity of aspect as the result of being seen through Essie's eyes rather than his own.

'Were you in Auckland long?' said Dan. He had been thinking of them together; and then Essie going away because of her diving.

'Only three years,' she said. 'I never did well in the national championships; not once in those three years. I don't know what it was. I was fine in preparation and in squad training; fine on tour, but I never even placed at the nationals. It sort of psyched me out in the finish, and I came back south and gave more time to other things.'

'You gave it up?'

'Not all at once. Oddly enough, for a couple of years I dived as well as ever, without much practice. I let it go though, it didn't run my life any more.'

'You'll always be a diver in my mind.' Dan thought of the way they had been: his attitudes and hers. He realized how selfish youth is: how covetous its loves, all sharp needs and expectations, all competition and comparison. His fierce determination to imprint both body and mind on young Essie; her equal will both to succumb and resist on her own terms. He watched Essie with her son, and he thought of his own daughters. There was a deep simplicity and directness in the love of a parent for child. Love between man and woman was complicated, fluctuating, strung with sexual tension and threat to the self.

His Essie. They see Dale at last, deceptively small amongst the other passengers from the ferry, wearing a yellow parka and soft shoes, and seeming amiable. But his eyes are dispassionate, dark, and he walks with masculine balance close to grace. 'Is this my reception committee,' he says. Dan hears himself giving a fatuous laugh, but Dale isn't interested in Dan. He looks at Essie with eyes that concentrate the focus of the evening, so that the slopping water of the berth, the miscellaneous people, the useless noise of life going on, disappear. The soft travelling bag slips from his fingers, and lies there at his feet.

'Hello Dale,' Essie says.

'Have you been all right?'

'I've been getting by.'

'Do you want money?' says Dale. He puts his hand inside his parka and brings out a stiff, bank paper bag. The edges of many notes are pressed like the pages of a new book.

'We've got all the money we need,' Dan says, and Dale looks at him for the first time; basalt eyes that could gut him anytime.

'Good for you,' says Dale quietly, as if Dan were a child interrupting the conversation of grown people to talk of his ice-block on a stick. And Essie gives a laugh which is not spiteful, but is quite impartial, and Dan realizes with anger and resolve, that she is not going to say anything to Dale to tell him how things are now; that she's watching to see what Dan can do. He competes, and nothing is ever said of it between them, but he grows more selfish because of it. He's disappointed in Essie there, as they walk on the darkening wharf, and the light reflected on the water undulates like a white sheet spread upon the surface.

'It's lazy weather,' said Essie. She relaxed in the faded deck chair. Her frilled blouse, so white amidst the garden colours, disguised the provocation of her figure. Dan poured more wine into her glass, and stood looking at her, and she closed her eyes, but smiled because she was aware of him. He bent and kissed her, and put his hands in her hair, then shifted them to glide beneath her blouse. The feel of her bra cups and the warm skin above them. He kissed her harder. 'Say,' she said, 'hold on,' and she turned her head. Dan followed her head and kissed her again; took his hand from her breasts, and held her shoulders. When the kiss was over, Essie laughed, and leant on his arm. The kissing had delayed their breathing, and excited them. 'You've found me in the mood for it,' said Essie.

'Let's go into the house then.'

'It's no use.'

'The best things are no use,' said Dan. He could feel the grass beneath his tender feet; through his hands he could feel the throb of Essie's pulse close to her neck.

'No, it's the time of the month,' said Essie with a smile and blush. 'You thought it was your lucky day,' she said.

'I still do,' said Dan. Richard came and put one hand on his mother's leg, and looked into her face, and spoke seriously in his own way. Dan sat down again next to them. He ran his fingers along the inside of Essie's other knee. 'I think it's a very lucky day,' he said.

'It's nice you say that.'

Richard sat down with his back against Dan's chair, and began picking grass and putting it on Dan's white foot. Dan slipped his watch from his wrist, and held it out to the boy so that it gleamed in the sun. 'You're disappointed,' said Essie. Dan spread the fingers of his hand on her knee to show that he didn't mind. 'I'll take my blouse off,' she said.

'I used to ask you to do that. You didn't like to in daytime.'

'I'm older now. I might as well while I can.' Essie undid the miniature buttons of her blouse, and took it off, and then her bra. 'Of course I breast fed Richard,' she said, in case Dan should see too great a change since she was a girl. The skin below her throat was lightly tanned and spread with a few freckles, but her breasts were very white, each tilted slightly to the side. The skin surrounding the nipples was roughened like orange peel, but the colour darker. 'I feel the slightest wind now,' Essie said. 'The skin being sensitive to it I suppose.' Just by her arm the fullness of the breast made a dart shaped crease so utterly feminine that for a moment Dan felt lust grip; but it passed, and left only appreciation and calm.

The longer they forbore mentioning wife and husband the clearer it became that neither would be talked of at all: not from any sense of guilt, in fact the opposite, from loyalty, for any reference made in that garden's mood would have a degree of disparagement or justification. Dan no longer wanted to go into Essie's house. He didn't want to see how her kitchen was, or what sort of books and wallpaper she and her husband chose. He only wanted to remember the garden with the winking berries, small, blemished apples of character, things cheerfully overgrown, and the elm as king there, crepe yellow against the wall and the sky. Essie was lying back with her eyes closed; naked to the waist in the sun. The skirt band was tight enough to hold back the slight forward curve of her belly. 'Why is it rather sad though, Essie, to meet again?' he said.

'You just realize you're not young any more,' said Essie matter of factly. She didn't open her eyes. She brushed one breast at the feel of an insect, and the flesh trembled.

'We used to go fishing,' said Dan.

'Once or twice. That's all surely.'

'We did. We did though. We quite often went fishing from the rocks of the Cape. We caught fish too: cod mainly. You used to wear jeans and a yellow, ribbed jersey.'

'What, always? You've remembered it often perhaps, but we only went once or twice. Unless it was some other girl.'

'Come on. We gave fish to your parents. I remember that as well.'

'We buried them when you'd gone,' said Essie. They laughed together, and Essie opened her eyes to look at him, and help up the palm of her hand to shield herself from the glare of the sun. 'Mum thought they might be diseased,' she said. 'They didn't look like the clean fillets she was used to from the shops.'

'More disillusion,' said Dan. 'I liked your mother.'

His Essie. She stands with her back to the cold wind that presses with an even force from the bay. 'You know I need to go to Auckland,' she says. 'I need to move there if I'm going to have a chance to improve any more, and do any good.' Even in that grey, eroded day she is handsome and strong. Her dark hair is shaped close to her face; short for her diving, and the high neck of her red jersey is folded to her throat. 'You can come too. You could come up and get a job there, so things would be the same. But we've been over and over it all, you know that.'

'I can't come,' he burst out. 'I can't just toss in here, and hope to get the sort of job I want again. And why should I.' Why should he? Why should he have to follow her when she wasn't prepared to stay for him. Why should he — and he wouldn't; for once she put herself first and he acquiesced then so it would go on and on. And things wouldn't be the same, and he doesn't want things the same anyway: he wants them different, but the manner of the difference he can't explain.

'I mightn't be there all that long,' she says.

'Oh, come on. Once you're up there, that's it isn't it.'

'Your choice. I've made mine,' says Essie. She deliberately looks away from him; looks over to a group running on the cold sand and towing their scarves in the wind; looks there to show him that he isn't all the world by any means, that it and she will go on no matter what he does.

'Bloody marvellous, isn't it,' he says. As well as what is said, each of them makes private decisions. Each withdraws one more means of access to the heart.

In Essie's garden Dan had talk of personal things. He thought how often the enduring sweet or bitter experiences are of no relevance much to formal memory. The image of Essie diving; the taste of crayfish, and the colour of their scalded armour; pine roots as veins in clay banks; the scent of lupins and sand-dunes and fennel. The emotions of his life were strung on such things.

'Tell me things you remember we did together,' said Dan. So Essie talked of dances rather than fishing trips, of eccentricities rather than lovemaking. He could smell the warm, bleached canvas of his deck chair as he listened. Some of her recollections were only half familiar to him, and needed her sense of actuality to convince him that they had happened at all. Essie's memories were all good times it seemed, and Dan was reluctant to leave them, or the sunlit garden in which they were shared.

'Don't bother to put on your shoes again,' said Essie. 'Who's to know, if you don't get out of the car.'

'Ah, too much wine and sun and reminiscence,' said Dan. He swayed, having stood up abruptly. Essie slipped her blouse on without caring about the buttons, and went to the gate of the walled garden with him. Her sleek breasts were only partly hidden by the lace. 'Essie, let's hope not to see each other again,' said Dan. 'But life's not like that. I don't expect another time it will go as well.'

'Why not?'

'We won't be alone again like this; or just with Richard at this age.'

'I think it would be good to meet again,' said Essie. 'Our whole families even.'

There was rank mint by the gate. Dan took some as he said good-bye to Essie, and before he closed the car door he crushed the leaves vigorously in the palm of one hand with the heel of the other before dropping them. As a genteel lady might, he lifted his hand to his face to catch the scent of mint as he drove. The sun was crouching, still insistent, and Dan had the window down and drove into the city with bare feet and his trousers rolled up below the knee. He understood his Essie was gone, even from Essie herself: that the Essie he'd spent the afternoon with had grown wonderfully out of his Essie — but wasn't the same. His quick, vivid and sometimes angry Essie was lost except in memory. There he could see her still, yet never catch a glimpse of his own self. No former self to place with his Essie; just the ache of his presence having been with her then.

He drove into the hot city in the late afternoon. He had the window down, his trousers rolled up, his shirt undone to let the air stir the hair of his chest; and the scent of mint from his hand. He was dishevelled and relaxed. He let go; he forgave; he allowed some things to slip away, and was the better for it. But he kept an image of the new Essie in her rough, summer garden: and an image of his Essie, quick and strong in the air as she dived from a height towards him.

Wyldebaume
At the Frontier

I (persona rather than alter-ego) had worked part-time in the old Clerks' Room at Laystall, Zimmermann, Laystall and Clone, and never once took my shoes off, although it was a mosque for some, and never once had Zimmermann come in; he dealt with those in the main office. (What I did, or was paid to do, in the Old Clerks' Room I will imagine later so as not to detract from the forward movement of this opening section.) Then on a heatwave Thursday: the specific gives an impression of verisimilitude: I took my shoes off just that once because my feet were sweating — and Zimmermann entered the Old Clerks' Room.

> **epithalamium**, *n.* (*pl.* **-ums,-a**). Nuptial song or poem. (GK *thalamos* bride-chamber)

I swear to you — if legal identification is possible in our form of contact — it's absolutely true: not a word of a lay. I was caught out in the open by the paper cabinet getting some of the quarto size light yellow correspondence quality paper headed in green — Laystall, Zimmermann, Laystall and Clone. Solicitors, Barristers, Notaries Public, and so on with the address.

> And the frogs of the old quarry had their say too, like stair boards underfoot. *(Notebooks, March '83)*

I could smell my own feet; that sugary smell of hot feet in socks. To Zimmermann it must have been much stronger. It's a biological fact you see, that you have a diminished receptivity to your own smells. Despite the heat and his recent marriage (a necessary touch to allow the introduction of epithalamium, and also suggest carnality) Zimmermann wore an elegant, grey suit and blue suede waistcoat. And as an affectation, on both our parts, he sported a fob watch on a plain, oh so heavy silver chain; like a Pumblechook perhaps, or an Old Jolyon. He took the watch from his fob pocket, and held it cautiously in his hand, with his thumb arched above it lest like a toad it make sudden leap and escape. Zimmerman's mouth opened, his mouth and tongue glistened, as if he were about to begin an epithalamium, or perhaps it was just a reptilian tasting of the air.

A scout of Te Rauparaha, I edged towards my desk, socks gripping the stubble of residual carpet. There seemed just a possibility Zimmerman hadn't noticed, because the rest of me was fine; my tie knot for example still exemplary — snug in its collar.

> Laughing at himself with bitter and intense delight, as the profound Jester laughs at his own shadow crossed against the sky. *(Notebooks, April '86)*

'Wildbum,' said Zimerman,' take an obligatory two weeks notice.' I could see the toes of my brown shoes under the front of my desk — deserters who held their distance, and their tongues. Zimerman had addressed me perhaps ten times (nay not so much) in the three years, and his pronunciation of my name was always the same — he was attempting no insult. Oh, I could have told Zimerman the unlikely truth (could tell it to him now quite as easily), that I'd never taken off my shoes at work before, and that it is a coincidence, his coming in when I had, of about a thousand to one. But even if he were allowed to believe it, nothing would affect his assessment of the enormity of the error. As a parallel one (not the accusatory you, here) might as well put forward the first time excuse for rape.

Just on that Wildbum thing for a moment, it occurs to me that bum always suggests itself as unmistakably onomatopoeic, when it's not at all. Do you feel that same? Anyway to get back; quick as a flasher I decided not to take it lying down from Zimerman, but to unleash the dogs of pogrom. 'Zimerma,' I said, or perhaps 'Zimerma,' with just that altered, chilling inflexion. 'Zimerma, there comes a time in every man's life.'

Most of us are granted at least the blessing of never having to endure the death of our children. *(Notebooks, September '85)*

Zimerm's hand began to follow the silver chain towards the marsupial recluse of the yellow suede. I could feel the stubble of the Old Clerks beneath my Te Rauparaha souls, and for an instant as concentration heightened I was aware of a galaxy of dust particles tumbling and wheeling in the sun strip above the ribboned case files. Years of training — created in this instant — caused an automatic response. I pivoted with precise balance on my left foot, and drove the blade of my dexter hand for the single inch where the Dominus Cassurii nerve crosses the blunt bone of the Fenis Cooperum. I won't be apparent to you, but there's quite a pause here. I had typed Cooperii, altered it with twink, then compounded the error by typing over it too soon, and clogged the key of u. I cleaned it with an old tooth brush I keep in the second desk drawer. There was a packet of carrot seed there too — Manchester Table (Daucus Carota Sativa); a stump rooted variety suitable for all soil types, it says. The flesh, which is fine grained and free of core, is a deep orange colour.

'Wildbum, are you listening to me?' said Zimer. As it is my story you will have it on my terms or not at all. I'm not interested in what you expect, or have experienced. The Pharaohs concluded audience with their command — so let it be written; so let it be done. Not the reverse order, you will notice. Likelihood should never be a test of anything, for that is an appropriation of the freedom of others.

I briefly considered throwing myself on Zimer's mercy, but doubted it was sufficient to break my fall. For Zime was ambitious (and Zime was an honourable man). He wished to be a very Czar of David, and his gross ambition was betrayed by the faint, sugary aroma which persisted despite his toiletries.

Like that gaunt cat from the creek, I have begun to eat grass in order that death may be appeased. *(Notebooks, June '81)*

'What is the meaning of this, Wildbum?' said Zime. The meaning of this! I stand (shall we say) in my socks on the worn, commercial grade carpet in the Old Clerks' Room at Laystall, Zime, Laystall and Clone, the motes drifting in the pyramid light above the ribboned folders of a thousand animosities, and the great question is asked of me for immediate reply. What is the MEANING of, whatever. Wildbum, bum, bum, bum, bum — an echo is the beating of my heart. Beat, beat, beat, bum, bum, bum: the beat is to the heart of a different drum. Each genre must have a Fugleman.

I meant to say before, about my attitude to Zim and his ambition, that you're wrong to say (or to have said — but let's not tense up) that there's any ethnic rancour to the portrayal. No, NO, and there'll be no further interruptions in a summing up. You see, it's not that he's a Jew, but that he's a solicitor: an occupational not a racist prejudice. The one sign of validity in mass beliefs, is that all the world hates a lawyer.

> **ex cathedra** (ĕks kathē′dra, kă′thīdra) *adv.* & *a.* authoritative(ly); (of papal pronouncement) given as infallible judgement. [L, = from the (teacher's) chair]

So Zi fired me, there you are (where ARE you), and the instant had such significance it was caught in amber time; so that for eternity the silver watch chain glints, a shallow arc against the suede blue burnish, and the yellowed venetians in the Old Clerks' Room click ever so slightly like camels' teeth; the sound of Angela Pruitt typing in the main office is as the infantry in dispute at some remove, the tapping of both gunfire and courage beyond a no-man's land. My green shoes lie supine and reproachful as the heads of beaten dogs beneath the desk. There is perpetual spit to glaze Zi's pouched, red lip, and there is the sweet smell of my socks — or perhaps my life?

> **păd.** 1. n. Soft saddle; piece of soft stuff used to save jarring, raise surface, improve shape, fill vacant space, &c.; shin-guard in games; sheets of blotting or scribbling or drawing paper fastened together in a block; foot or sole of foot in hare, dog, &c.; (arch.) easy-paced horse. 2. v.t. (*-dd-*). Make soft, improve shape of, fill out, protect, with p. or pp. or padding; (sl.) *p. it* or *the hoof*, go on foot; *padded room* (for suicidal lunatic &c.). **pădd′-ing** n., (esp.) literary matter inserted merely to increase quantity. [ ]

So what have we arrived at, you and I, through the unexpected fracture of convenient effigii. Then in my socks, now in my cups, but fired by Z then and still fired by him today. The composite of things applying at any one time is always something of a process. There are nine tenses in our art, and only three in life. 'Wildbum, I mean what I say.' The entire point of the story is, of course, what happened *after*, which I'll get on to *now*. After, ah-h whatsisname, had fired me. You KNOW! The one with the camel's teeth and green suede waistcoat — I told you for christ's sake. Fair's fair; just hang on a bit, and it will come back to me.

> In my dream the wind is scented with fennel, and laughter drifts like a garland. The iris of the deep sky rolls round its pupil of earth and subtle ocean. *(Notebooks, December '77)*

Just where were we, or where was I? Is there anybody there? 'Wildbum, you are fired. Take an obligatory two weeks notice.' Is that the fellow we were talking about. Certainly I remember the feel of the stubble in the Old Clerks' Room, how the wood worm dust lies like pollen in the unused pigeon holes, and the sugary smell faint on the internal air. Do you know, the rest escapes me: perhaps you could tell me the story instead.

Babes and Brothers
In Arms

Frank preferred to sleep without any light, for sometimes in the dark he could believe he wasn't there; wasn't anywhere at all. The door of the hotel room, however, had a subdued courtesy light which Frank and Relda hadn't been able to turn off. Frank told her that it must be one of those things that they have in hotels now. 'Why were you laughing when we came up?' she said. Frank saw the outline of her head against the pillow of the other bed, and her arms close to her chest as always when she prepared to sleep. He wondered who she was; who she could be. He remembered that as a boy he had stolen communion wine on the night of an eclipse, and how he had lain in the sandhills of that strange world to drink it. The sweet wine in his mouth, the sand insubstantial beneath him, the moon closing an inner eyelid.

'Laughing?' he said.

'As we came up from the foyer you were laughing at something.'

He told her. A solemn man standing by the ferns had coughed, and like a small frog phlegm had sprung from his throat and landed on the reception desk. The man's solemn handkerchief had trapped it in an instant, as small frogs are trapped. 'I'm glad I didn't see,' said Relda.

'He coped so well.'

'I thought you were laughing at something about the reunion; something Margaret said probably.'

'Margaret and I didn't laugh much. She got stuck into me tonight about not being a good husband. Did she tell you that?'

'Take no notice,' said Relda. 'It's the split up with Tony of course, and coming to terms with it. She'll punish husbands in general for a while.' Frank hoped his wife wouldn't have the inclination to display Margaret's failed marriage to him again. Better to be left to recall the wine beneath an eclipse, or imagine the wonderful grain on a walnut clock case: better to just lie with his face away from the courtesy light and feel eventually he wasn't anywhere at all.

From the lookout they could see the lights of the city spread with the curve of the harbour; light against night. So many variations of colour and intensity; so many variations of movement and pulse. The city alight, and the dark harbour and sea beyond the Heads: the glitter and the void.

'How marvellous it all is though,' said Relda. 'I'd forgotten this view coming in by car at night.' She leant out eagerly over the wall of the lookout, as if a foot or two nearer to the city would bring something even more splendid into focus. 'Yes,' she said, 'I remember now, stopping just here and seeing it like this.' Frank experienced the odd combination of exasperation and envy which was his response to the tremulous sensitivity of his wife's reactions. She could still weep, despise and exult, while his assessment by intellect found increasing repetition.

'Quite a sight,' he said.

'We stopped sometimes; Margaret, Eileen and I,' said Relda, 'coming back to the Varsity and we'd see the city like this from the motorway.'

'Yes,' said Frank. He felt his interest and his thoughts slide away, despite his virtuous intentions. He felt isolation, as if passing into shadow.

'Margaret's determined to come, you know, even though they've parted for good. I admire her for not pulling back from things. It's not easy to come like this alone.'

'No.' As they went back to the car, he saw that they were the only ones who had stopped their night journey to view the city. They were solitary on the lookout area, and the lights of other cars flared in the dark, and quickly passed on the curve.

'This reunion,' said Frank.

'Yes?'

153

'A sign of the stage of life, a reunion. When people have developed a past; when they've grown wistful.'

'You'll know a few there, though. You'll know Harry and the ones I've kept in touch with.'

'I'll be fine,' said Frank. From the road afterwards there was no view of the city or harbour. The antithesis was lost of the city flowering in the night — and the dark sea. Just cars leaping past, markings flipping towards him as he drove, and the hills massed as clouds. 'You'll like to catch up on old friends,' he said.

'You don't mind coming?'

'I don't mind.' What appeared as consideration could be indifference. Frank drove more rapidly and the massed hills were a presence felt, though just shadow against shadow in the night.

As they lay in the hotel beds he had that feeling again; things sensed as gathering around him: not antagonistic, not sympathetic. The operation of forces distinct from human aspiration. A glimpse beyond that anthropomorphic guise men give nature to convince themselves that what they do has significance. Relda was talking of Margaret's marriage; leading him through Margaret's and Tony's life as if through their house: private emotions like lingerie upon an unmade bed, personal habits enumerated like the half-used medicines and salves in a bathroom cabinet. 'I'm not saying Margaret would be easy to live with, of course, but he can be a bastard of a man you know.' Frank had played sport with Tony for years, several times the four of them had gone on holiday together. Wasn't he eager to please, wasn't he a pleasant, hard-working, unexciting man who demanded little of his acquaintances? And now Frank knew all of his petty malice, his premature ejaculations, his sudden jealousies, the stuttering in his sleep, the separate account opened in secret. All the things in fact that one marriage partner trusts the other will never tell. The tortoise of self may be turned upon its shell so that the private parts are exposed in ignominy. 'He gave away some of Margaret's jewellery to his women. Stole some pieces from her, can you believe it, and gave them to women he took up with.' Everyone's life is the property of those who observe it; the motives for any action are imputed with superficial vehemence.

'Yes, that's mean,' said Frank.

'Her personal stuff like that.'

'Right,' said Frank. What things had he done, he wondered, that might pass from Relda sometime to some friend; pass to some other man lying in some other bed, who would feel the same mild contempt and pity, the same mild fear.

'My god,' said Margaret. 'Wine and cheese parties, eh, Frank.' She stayed talking with him after Relda had sighted friends, and been drawn off.

'At a wine and cheese there comes a thought that you weren't considered significant enough to be invited to what really mattered; more substantial fare for the inner man and inner circle.'

'I'm not going to start talking about Tony and me,' Margaret said. She didn't look like a desperate divorcee. She looked the same shrewd, married woman. Shrewd, yes, was how she looked.

'I don't mind.'

'I was thinking of myself,' said Margaret. 'Oh, you could stand it all right, but could I?' Frank could see his wife smiling, and listening to Harry Grobner. Briefly he could see her, as the wildebeest of the wine and cheese party shifted ground. She looked hopeful, trusting, and forty years old. 'Who are you looking for?' said Margaret.

'Relda.'

'Or that woman in purple. Relda's drinking up large tonight, Frank, have you noticed that? I'd say you might have a few home truths before the night is out. A few home truths — something to look forward to. Mind you this bulk wine is evil enough to wring a confession of treason from man or beast.'

'That girl in purple, I see what you mean.' It was a ploy, and he didn't really care if it succeeded or not.

'Oh, I know she's got a very nice bum and tits. That's what you men go for isn't it? Are you a bum and tits man, or do you like thigh and leg. Each sexual appetite must have its preference known.'

'I don't dine out enough to establish favourites.'

'That's witty,' said Margaret. 'Yes, very good. Well Tony found his opportunities, and you may in time, though I'd say work was your obsession. You don't know a great deal about Relda, do you? You haven't a clue why she's really here, and you don't much care to find out. You're a cold fish; always have been. A cold, sad fish, Jesus save us. So why do you think Relda's been such a great mother, such a support of the Hospice League, so soft-hearted for pets, christmas time, daytime television. She spends herself on famines and flowers, on shampoos of jasmine, on crock pots with cheerful, orange patterns.'

Maybe other conversations in those busy rooms were less casual than they seemed. Maybe the eyes strayed as Frank's did, because home truths there too were being served with feigned reluctance or convinced equanimity. Frank attempted to feel indignation, but only disappointment as ever was provided. Margaret saw it as her duty to give it to him straight: to be frank, as it were. 'Do you know why she came; why you're booked in at that hotel?' Frank had no reply to prompt her, but she had the answers herself. 'No, you don't know, because you've never cared enough to find out how Relda feels. She came with Garrick Hall when they were engaged, and they had the curtains open in the night, she told me, so that they could see the stars from the bed.' Margaret was looking up at his face; looking up to feed on his response, the emotion in his face, but he kept his expression mild and non-committal. He understood that malice was usually an outcome of unhappiness; that it had more reference to its origin than to its object. 'They were together here,' said Margaret.

'First love is romantic,' he said.

'Poor old Relda,' Margaret said. 'No wonder she still has to think of some hotel night when the stars shone. I've needed to say something to you for Relda's sake for a long time, and recently I've become tough enough to do it. Tell you what a detached, selfish bastard you are.'

Pale and shiny was the cheek ridge of Relda's face, in the light which couldn't be turned off. Her night cream gave the skin the gloss of tears, and the line of one eyebrow seemed a feather against paleness. 'All in all,' she said, 'they're better off apart.'

'I suppose you're right,' Frank said.

'Not that it's easy. It's not an easy thing after so many years, whether for the best finally or not.' She sounded very sure, as if she had given considerable thought to it.

When he was young, all adults seemed secure in an equal confederacy of wisdom and ritual, but when grown up himself he found that there was no special fraternity of adults, and no necessary security. Fools, and the unlucky, persisted in their roles; the capable prospered; the rest coped as best they could.

'It's more Eileen that I'm concerned about,' said Relda. 'She's stuck in that hospital; having been told what she's been told, and just has to deal with it.' Frank had dreams sometimes which woke him in a state of desperation: goading dreams; innuendos of compacts broken, portents overlooked, necessary actions and responsibilities neglected. Nothing specific enough to be acted upon. His body produced a range of symptoms that could be selectively grouped to fit some of the worst ways to go. He had observed the bowl to see if his stools floated or sank, and then could not remember which was the desired augury. 'I found it difficult to talk to Danny Fougerie,' said Relda. 'Isn't that strange. When we worked together, he was one that I got on very well with. It always had to do with the job though, I suppose, for I realised tonight that we had nothing else in common. A little embarrassing for us both I think, but then others came and rescued me.'

Relda seemed to Frank to be happy talking to her friends from years before, or just as intimately to their husbands and wives met only that evening. She had that warmth and well intentioned curiosity concerning the lives of others, that women often have. Frank stood with Harry and a lecturer in Russian. The recitation of other people's lives dismayed him almost as completely as the contemplation of his own life dismayed him: the repetition, the predictability, the selfishness and transience of it all. Harry departed to continue his tasks as host; supplying drinks and humour as he moved. The Russian explained the scope of his investments, and Frank squeezed up his eyes, and punctuated the other's talk with grunts which could be affirmation or derision. Frank disliked long discussions concerning money even more than talk of people's personal lives, and not just because he wasn't wealthy. He recognised the utility of money as he recognised the utility of keeping his body clean, yet he didn't wish to discuss the details of either. The Russian spoke of Commercial Bills on the short term investment market. Such was his urgency and conviction that he felt compelled to put his hand on Frank's arm, as if to prevent him from taking a drink and so being distracted. Frank would rather have talked of the Père David deer restored at last to China from the Woburn Abbey estate;

a lost species seen again at the old Nanhaizi hunting park. But when he found the opportunity to do so, the lecturer just said it was odd how things worked out; asked how Frank's glass was, and went to fill his own. He smiled and laughed, and kept putting distance between himself and Frank.

It takes energy to be socially receptive, and Frank was tiring. He made a search of the rooms, and found a bottle of reasonable wine put aside by Harry until the casks had been emptied. Frank opened his prize quietly at the drinks table, then went out and sat on the steps. There is a measure of aimlessness and artificiality to most parties, casual social contact must be expected to produce them, but Frank was not depressed. Provided that he wasn't compelled to make or suffer much conversation himself, he was tolerant of the involvement of others. He drank the satisfactory wine, and enjoyed the cooling movement of the night air. There were ragged hedges which cast shadows like breakers on the lawns, and moths in a bumbling process of soft disintegration. Laughter sometimes escaped the compacted murmur from within the building, rose up and was gone above the shadows and hedges. Frank wondered how the engagement between Garrick Hall and Relda had ended, and what other things Margaret could tell him that his wife would not.

'Do you want me to come in?' said Relda from the other bed. She had been watching him perhaps. It was always her back to front way of asking.

'Do you want to?'

'Yes.' She was sitting up.

'Come on then,' he said, and Relda came quickly across, and folded the sheet neatly at her chin.

'That's better,' she said.

In time a natural vantage point is reached from which something of a panorama can be seen, nothing spectacular, and you admit to yourself that this is what life is. This is all of it. Although the outcome of events is not predictable, the components are ever the same — just vanity, success, and the pain, disappointment, apprehension and wistfulness you already know. And if the limits are imposed from without, or arise from your own deficiencies, the result is still the same. This is all of it, after all.

'You're sad, aren't you,' Relda said.

'I don't think so.'

'You're always sad when anything special happens. When we go anywhere, or old friends come to see us. You're sad if the routine is broken; sad to add to the things no longer left to happen. It's odd in you that.' Frank had no denial, for any positive experience emphasises the passage of time. Things transient; half worn away before they're over. The falling cadence becomes stronger until the visible pulse behind each smile and conversation, each leavetaking and return, behind promises and beliefs, is the identical pulse of time's movement, like the throb a bus has on a prolonged night journey along the coast.

Frank brought Relda coffee after coming back inside. 'You okay?' he said.

'I've been talking to Isobel. Eileen's got cancer. I knew she was sick, but not that. She weighs six stone, Isobel says, and she cried when she wasn't well enough to come tonight. She sent a card, and Isobel's taped it on the door. Come and look.' She took his hand, and went before him through the people. 'I'm showing Frank poor Eileen's card,' she told a shiny faced man who blocked her way, and he dropped his shoulders in apology and moved aside. Eileen had written on the plain card in green ink, *Have a wonderful reunion. I'm there everyway I can. Talk about me too.*

'Six stone; six stone.' Relda's voice was just a whisper. Her hand tightened on his. Frank wondered when it would be his turn to write a green plea upon a card, and was ashamed of his selfishness, and yet kept thinking about it. He had obscure pains sometimes in his groin, and he tired easily. Specks drifted often in his vision like gnats, and threatened reality. 'Talk about me too, she says,' said Relda. 'Let's talk about her, Frank. Shall we?'

'All right.' He knew that if he started, she would soon go on. 'Once she came to stay, soon after we were married, and stood by our kitchen window laughing at Hansen the curate next door, who wore overalls to mow the lawn, and held pegs in his mouth while he put out the washing.'

'That's right,' said Relda with delight. She took up the recollections of Eileen, as he knew she would. Harry came with a wine cask, filling glasses, taking other glasses away for spirits, and a man half-turned to Frank in a nearby group had a warm, catchy laugh. Frank liked to hear it, though he was too far to know its cause. Eileen had loved to laugh. There is an element of irony in all enjoyment: Eileen would be aware of that. Frank tried to imagine her six stone. Some things are absurd because of their appearance, like very fat women in suspender belts; some things are absurd because of their names, like axolotl and Schleswig-Holstein; some by their nature, like poets and caretakers. Frank supposed there must be humour of some kind in six stone, and humour also in his full body-weight weekend.

'If you pull the curtains back, we could see the stars,' said Relda. So Frank left the bed and did it. As Relda and Margaret and Garrick all knew, the stars could be clearly seen. Frank lay and watched them. He knew that Relda was crying, although there were no sobs. 'That card on the door,' she said, 'and no Eileen.' Her voice was higher and her body very still. Tears would be the only movement; moles in the night.

'I'm sorry about Eileen,' he said. Tears for the way Eileen was dying. Tears for her own life with him, and for the recollection of Garrick Hall perhaps in the same hotel; brighter stars and the fragrance of a young, strong man. 'Don't cry. Don't cry,' Frank said into her shoulder.

'I'm not,' she said, and he could almost feel the tears moving. 'Eileen was so sharp,' she said. 'So sharp and honest.' Now sharpened a good deal more; whittled to a barb that would pierce the everyday and escape. And Garrick had been sharp no doubt, in youth and a Van Gogh starry night.

Frank laid an arm over his wife so that his hand rested by her hands. 'Think of all the good things of the evening,' he said. 'Margaret and Harry, and all the others you've met again.' He thought that his arm away from his body might feel to her like some other arm. He wanted her to be happy, and as he couldn't ensure that himself, why not inhabit her memory as another.

'Some I really wanted to see weren't there.' They were close and separate, looking to the sky. Frank felt the focus of her energy move away from him. All the time between one visit and the next could be a wintering over of emotions. He could understand the lure; the power of her recollection, for in every man is a yearning for a woman he hasn't wounded. He could wish to be her love.

The stars reminded him of the milk white peacock of the poem. Such huge stars at such distance that they could barely be seen. Frank thought about how a star can be seen for ages after it has ceased to exist: how an image may persist when substance is gone.

A Poet's Dream
Of Amazons

My friend Esler is sick again. His mother rang, and implored me to hurry to the bed-side. She spoke in a whisper, not in deference to the sinking Esler, but from fear that her husband might overhear. Mr Esler hates me.

'He says he mightn't see the night out,' said Mrs Esler. 'He's had a dream again about a Big Woman, and she turned out to be a preammunition of death.' Mrs Esler is loyal in her way, but for a mother of that son her vocabulary is less than impressive. 'The doctor's been twice already,' she whispered. I suppose that a really Big Woman, and irrational as women often are in dreams, could quite well be a sinister omen.

I put down my work at once. I knew it was no joke if Esler said he was dying: well rather I knew that he might laugh about it, but die all the same. Esler fights a persistent and terrible battle against the world, but it is a losing battle.

My moped was in the shed, but before opening the door to it, I rattled the neighbours' fence to start their dog barking. A melancholy and majestic sound that dog made: deep bells in the cold air. Why should anyone sleep if Esler was dying? I interspersed the hound's barks with appeals to Odin, the god of my ancestors. I didn't want Esler to die, for he is one who speaks my language in this town.

On my moped I set a course from the forlorn suburb in which I lived, to the forlorn suburb in which Esler lived. Mrs Esler was watching for me: she was at the door when I approached, hoping that she would be able to smuggle me through to the laundry without

a confrontation with her husband. I saw half of him in the doorway
of the living room; one arm, one side, one leg, one eye looking
down the passage to the front door, and half a sneer to have seen a
grown man arrive on a fifty cc step-thru. 'It's only you,' said Mrs
Esler. She pulled a face. 'The doctor's been twice. Oh, it's bad, it's
bad.' She made another sudden face. Pulling faces is the qualifier
Mrs Esler uses when her husband is at hand. They are the briefest
flashes across her long face; semaphore by tic which hint at the
hospitality, gratitude and compassion she can't speak of. They are
spasms of emotional intent, and probably quite unconscious. 'You
can't stay long,' she said, as we went up the passage, and then a
fleeting contortion to nullify her tone. 'Mr Esler and I don't want
you coming around really,' she said, and touched my arm. I turned
at the laundry door, and went back, and put my head into the living
room. I could see the back of Mr Esler's head as he watched sport
on the television. There was a worn patch at the crown, as if he had
a habit of twisting his head into the pillows at night.

'Mr Esler.'

'Uh,' said Mr Esler.

'I'm going through to see Branwell.' I said it loudly so that it
would carry to Esler in his bed.

'Oh, it's you,' said Mr Esler. He didn't turn towards me.

Esler had his blue tartan dressing gown on in bed. He looked bad
enough to be dying, but he was trying to laugh. He flipped his
hands on the covers, and further down I could see his feet jerk.
'Branwell. Branwell,' he wheezed. 'I love it,' As well as liquid at
the corners of his eyes, there was white gathered there, like a little
toothpaste. On his cheeks were patterns from the creases in the
pillow. Esler is balder than his father, but in a different way; going
back a long way at the temples, and the hair between quite downy.
'Branwell's good,' he said, 'and look!' He put his hand under the
pillow and produced a flat bottle of brandy. 'You see before you
indeed, the Earl of Northangerland.'

Esler's voice was squeezed out, as if someone was sitting on his
chest. The Big Woman perhaps. His wrist buckled with the effort
of getting the brandy bottle back under his pillow. I'd thought up
the mention of Branwell as I went over; something to give Esler a
lift. He becomes depressed without literary allusions from time to

time. He began to tell me about his fantasy of the Big Woman. 'As did the Pharoah I have a dream,' said Esler. 'Each night this vast and determined woman comes to wrestle with me.'

'All I get are nightmares of rooms without doors, and sinking ground beneath my feet.'

'Night after night,' said Esler, 'she seeks me out, and we must love and fight.'

Esler's room had been the laundry, but his mother now has an automatic washing machine in the old pantry, alongside the deep-freeze. The laundry tubs have been taken out, and Esler's bed moved in; and a small table by the window. Esler's boyhood room has become a guest room; which means it's never used. His father refuses to let Esler keep it because he is thirty-six years old, a poet, and still at home. Living in the laundry is one of those strange and bitter compromises that families have, and which remain incomprehensible to outsiders.

Mrs Esler came and interrupted her son just when he was describing to me the body lock that the naked Big Woman put on him in their struggle. All poets have a tendency to pornography. 'Mr Esler says you've started him coughing again. He won't have it.' Her lengthening face, pulled inexorably towards the grave, convulsed to disavow the message she delivered. When she left, Esler continued to tell me of his Big Woman: a giant poster nemesis of sex. It was typical of Esler that even those things threatening his very life, could only appear ludicrous.

His room retains a faint smell of soap and washed woollens. A fine mould like candle smoke covers the underside of the window sill, residue from a more tropical climate.

'Is he still there?' shouted Mr Esler. He must have been taking advantage of an injury stoppage on the television.

'Night after night she comes; this immense woman,' wheezed Esler. 'Hair like a waterfall, navel a labyrinth, thighs like a wild mare.' Esler's warm breath had scents of meatloaf, medication and mortality. His gums had shrunk from the palings of his teeth.

Esler's clothes are on plastic hangers on nails along the laundry wall opposite his bed, and his books are heaped beneath on shelves made from bricks and planks. What can I tell you of my friend which won't make you feel contempt or pity. What can I tell you of this man who is better than us; whose interests and principles have made him in a modern world a mockery; whose skills are as little considered as those of a thatcher or a messiah.

'Waikato have scored again,' shouted Mr Esler, and Mrs Esler made an odd sound of wifely concurrence, like the instinctive response of a duck to another's call.

Esler and I have been friends since we ganged up at eleven to beat the second largest boy in the class: a prematurely hairy slob who used to hold us under water during swimming periods. We became one of those braces so common amongst boys — Brunner and Esler. We heard our names coupled more at school than we heard them separately. I can imagine the staffroom association.

'Caned Brunner today.'

'Who?'

'Brunner. Fair haired kid; hangs about with Esler. Caned him too.'

Or perhaps, 'That's Esler isn't it, smashing those milk bottles?'

'No, that's Brunner.'

'Both look the same to me, little buggers. Call him over.'

We fought together, smoked together, marvelled at the sky and stars together, took out the O'Reilly girls together. I have a scar on the underside of my left arm because Esler accidentally shot me with a home-made spear gun. We both saw Bushy Marsden collapse and die in the gym. We began the dangerous experiment of taking words seriously, and so resisting the process of attrition by which life betrays us.

'The Big Woman has a scent of almonds and macrocarpa,' said Esler in wonder and dread. His tartan wool dressing gown is also his lucky writing jacket, ever since he had it on when he wrote his Van Gogh sequence. Constant use without washing, a little lost food and the oils of feverish sweat from his asthma bouts, have taken the nap from it, have buffed it until it shines like silk, and the original tartan pattern is almost lost. 'Read me something to take my mind off breathing,' said Esler. He had a hundred poets to choose from, and I read Seamus Heaney to him. He nodded his downy head and squeaked 'Yes, yes,' at the touches which moved him. The liquid and the white gathered at the extremes of his eyes; spread a little to the corner skin.

'Will you stop that never ending jawing in there,' shouted Mr Esler to me.

'Exactly,' Mrs Esler said. I could almost hear the snap as her face, just for a moment, was contrite, bewildered.

'Read on,' said Esler.

The laundry never seems a bedroom no matter how long Esler is in it, or how many clothes or books he lines the wall with. Images of soap flakes linger in the air as a false christmas, and one corner of the lino always seems to be damp. There is more utilitarian aura than even poetry can dispel. 'That's so,' said Esler as I read. In a paper packet on the second plank are one hundred and seventy three green copies of Esler's poems printed by the Whip-poor-will Co-operative Press. I have the dedication by heart: *These poems are for Bruce Brunner and Frank Heselstreet, fellow poets and friends who share my belief that emotion is like ours a round world, and as far enough east becomes west, so is laughter to tears and genius to insanity.*

I have eighteen copies in the top of my wardrobe. Frank and I buy one from the bookstore when we can afford to, and have our reward later when Esler tells us of another green pamphlet sold. Frank says we might end up with the whole edition of Esler's poems: a private joke, but what are friends for. Esler has always been absurd, but it is only one trait of character; as is deceit or shrewdness, composure or ambition. Just one aspect of my friend, but it makes it difficult to decide if he is dying or not. In a way I understand the Grim Reaper concluding that it is below his dignity to come for Esler; and sending a very Big Woman instead, who can laugh in her killing work and not be out of character.

Mr Esler appeared at the laundry door. His face was like that of a rock groper: reactionary and full of low cunning. 'You're doing him no good at all. Leave him alone can't you. I blame you for a lot of it,' he said. I never resent Mr Esler's antagonism. I see it rather as one of the few remaining signs of concern for his son — this determination to blame me.

'I know you do,' I said.

'How many did Waikato win by?' said Esler in his squeezed voice. His father knew that Esler didn't care, but couldn't deny himself the satisfaction of saying the score out loud.

'Thirty two, ten,' he said. 'Thirty two bloody ten.'

'That means a season's tally so far of one hundred and forty two for, and fifty three against,' said Esler. 'How many did Mattingly score?'

'Fifteen.'

'That makes him the highest scoring Fullback in Waikato provincial rugby apart from Rawiri,' said Esler.

'You don't care. You don't care!' shouted his father.

'It's so though,' said Esler. He didn't care, but it was so though. He spent fifteen or twenty minutes each day on rugby statistics so that he could know more than his father and still disregard the game.

Mr Esler knew better than to dispute Esler's facts; instead he looked around the laundry as a rock groper does another's cave. 'This place stinks of idleness,' he said.

'Mattingly has twenty four points to go before he reaches Rawiri's record, and he's already played three more first class games,' said Esler. His voice became treble with an effort at volume as his father left.

'Shut up,' cried Mr Esler from the passage.

'Each night now she comes, my Amazon,' said Esler. 'Beautiful, but so huge. Dear god. I try to oppose her with intellect and poetry when lust has failed. It's no use. She's killing me, the Big Woman; ending me with breasts and kisses.' Esler cleaned his lips by rubbing them with his fingers, and concentrated on breathing well for a time.

'I've never been afraid of women, or been against women, have I,' he said.

'I know.'

'The power, the weight, yet the subtleness of her. I can't stand it.'

'Take a sleeping pill or something,' I said.

'I can't. Not with my regular medication.'

Esler is loyal and honest; totally without envy or malice in his friendship, perhaps because the only basis he knows for friendship now is poetry. I have watched his other means of communication atrophy. Esler can discuss anthropomorphic imagery with wit and eloquence for hours, but when the grocer questions him of necessities,

167

Esler grips the counter, is helpless before yet another stranger, stumbles to tell of sliced bread or free flow green beans. People exchange glances and knowing smiles at this evidence of the dangers inherent in any serious scrutiny of the mind. Esler tries to give Frank and me money from his savings account which has less than three figures: he writes to the *Listener* to point out that regional poets Brunner and Heselstreet have not received sufficient recognition. He is ugly, incongruous, annoying, ludicrous; and a true friend.

Esler asked me to bring a packet from the laundry table. 'It's my new poems to go to Australia,' he said. 'I want you to post it for me: you're luckier than me. Bless it before you put it in the box.' He made no mention of the postage charge: such things are incidental when you are dying. 'Send it airmail, and don't let them use any stamps with heads on. They're unlucky for manuscripts, I always feel.' All the seams in the brown paper were traced with sellotape, and the parcel was quartered in string woven of green and red strands. I bet Esler had said a prayer or a curse over his parcel, and sprinkled on some of the lucky dust that he'd collected from beneath Honey McIlwraith's bed. Esler is that sort of intellectual and innocent. He really believes that there could be someone out there interested in poetry, willing to publish or pay for it, someone who will untie Esler's two tone string, unpick his sellotape — and cry genius.

'If the Big Woman comes again tonight,' said Esler, then trailed off and began wheezing. It became worse until he was flapping his shoulders, and his veins began to swell.

'Puffer, puffer,' called his mother as she ran in. Her face twitched to one side then the other, as if offering her endless christian cheeks to be slapped. She meant the asthma gadget with the diaphragm, and she and I tugged Esler to a sitting position, and she did his throat thoroughly, as if to ensure it would remain free of greenfly.

When he felt easier, Esler lay back again. 'Okay mum, okay,' he said. 'I'm fine now.' He turned away from us until he could regain the personal distance he required after the ignominy of his attack, his weakness, his mother with the puffer. Mrs Esler touched his downy head once, but he turned more resolutely, and she went out: first her dull curls and then the rest of her face, feature by feature, as a freight train curves from view. Esler rested: his skin gleamed with the sweat of illness and puffer liquid. I watched the soap flakes, and the light of the moon through the window without any curtain.

'Where's Frank?' said Esler finally.

'In Wellington at the technicians' course,' I said.

'They'll destroy him in the end, those computers,' he said. 'He left me the last poem in his Scheherazade series. So detached; so nimble. It makes me doubt my own progress. But those computers are the danger for poor Frank.' He picked up his puffer, held it to his mouth, but forgot to use it. Instead he said, 'I wish I could have a civilized life.' Beneath the bottom plank of his bookcase, close to the bricks, are Esler's two pairs of shoes. Brown shoes with roughly sewn seams, and each left heel worn to a slant, and the inside liners curling up. Where the outlets for the tubs had pierced the wall, Eslcr has fitted wooden plugs covered with muslin to improve the seal.

'Pass the ball; pass it!' cried his father from the living room.

'France,' said Esler, looking at his poets gathered on the planks. 'France has always seemed to me a place where people have a civilized life.'

'A cultivated people. A people who accept without reserve the necessity of art,' I said. I had almost starved to death on my one sojourn there. Having been nowhere, Esler still believed that life can be essentially different in other parts of the world.

He began on the Big Woman again. He was amused by his own recollections of the dreams. It was a tribute to his creative impulse that even the thing he thought was killing him was transmuted into an entertainment for us both. He had his brandy bottle in one hand, his puffer in the other, and he was trying not to laugh. 'You know,' he said, 'the odd thing is that I do feel that I might be dying this time after all. It's more than asthma the doctor said; but he doesn't know about the Big Woman of course.'

Later he started tossing about. I put his brandy away and called his mother. She began to fuss over him, but he became worse. Mrs Esler called to her husband that he'd have to ring the doctor about Esler needing to go into hospital, and Mr Esler came and stood by the bed. He has a face not wildly dissimilar to our own: eyes facing forward, a two-entry nose, mouth, and teeth still nominally intact.

Yet what a gulf of species is there. He might as well have been a rock groper or a pear tree standing in the laundry.

'Thirty-six years old, writing bloody poetry, still has asthma, and now dirty dreams,' he said. 'Jesus.' The sound of the puffer was loud. 'I blame you,' he said to me.

'So do I,' said Mrs Esler, her face hidden.

'Heckel and bloody jeckel. It was a sorry thing when you two and that Frank Heselstreet met up,' said Mr Esler. He went out to phone the doctor.

I decided to go the back way. Mrs Esler came out with me. At the other end of the hall I could see Mr Esler with the telephone cord drawn tight. That way he could stand at the living room door and watch the television as he waited to get through to the doctor.

'This asthma can't be all that serious can it?' I asked Mrs Esler. 'I mean he's had bouts before and come through. There's nothing else is there?' Mrs Esler held her nose to stop herself from crying, and I didn't say any more. She gave a final, ambiguous face, and then turned her interminable chin away. Mr Esler talked at the other end of the passage on his extended line, as Mrs Esler went back into the laundry.

For a time I waited in the moonlight of winter outside the Eslers' back door. What it came down to I suppose, was that I thought my friend Esler couldn't die because nothing was ready; and because it wasn't just. There was still too much that was ludicrous, and too much confusion. But you and I and Esler can't always rely on an appropriate setting for our deaths. Esler might have to go in a laundry bed, with soap flakes in the air, brandy under the pillow, a puffer in his mouth, and a Big Woman squeezing him in his dreams; with mould like candle smoke beneath the window sill, with one green vanity collection of his poems from the Whip-poor-will Press, with a polished blue, tartan dressing gown, and no reason for it to be happening at all. And just a friend or two, who can do nothing but remember better times.

As I walked the path at the side of the house, Mr Esler leant excessively from his window to bring his harsh whisper closer to me. 'Murderer,' he hissed. 'Don't come back. Leave him alone. You bloody writers have done for him.' The moon struck down, and held the Eslers' garden in a frost of light. I didn't take the accusation too much to heart. I knew Mr Esler becomes desperate late at night when all the sports programmes end; when he finds himself with hours ahead and no team left to join, and none to hate; just his wife's Greek faces and his son in the laundry with the ailments of asthma and poetry.

'Murderer,' I heard Mr Esler hissing. There were guilty ones of course: Pound and Olson, Eliot and Larkin, Yeats and Frost, Stevens and Neruda, Lowell and Williams, Turner and Sewell, had all made their attacks on Esler. And Dylan Thomas. Now there's a murderer if ever I read one.

At the end of Te Tarehi Drive, and turning into Powys Street, which lay stark in the moonlight, I couldn't help laughing at the dying Esler. Laughter can be a guise of love: laughter can be helplessness expressed. Perhaps Esler is simply dying of his poets' amazement at the world in which he finds himself.

I let the moped engine run on in the shed for a few minutes, so that the battery would charge up a bit after the light had been on. I shook the neighbours' fence to rouse Cerberus again, and savoured the echoing sound. A deep barking dog suits a full moon. Esler had been dying before; and got over it. We all have to get over a little dying of ourselves in life. Is he dying of the asthma and the other things his mother wouldn't say: or is the Big Woman, that preammunition of death, suffocating him in his dreams with excess of loving?